Him, Me, and V

Based on a true story of child abuse, survival, and healing.

Amy Joy

Little Daisies Publishing, LLC

Disclaimer

This is our story, mine and the ones who grew up with *Him*. Many details and identifying information have been changed to protect those who may look for themselves among these pages. Our story is ours alone and no one else's story is told here. Because much has been altered to protect myself and others, this book is *based on a true story*, not a true memoir.

The heart of a child wants simple things like love, warmth, sunshine: to be seen. I did experience these things but in separate corners of my life, weekends mostly, and with those who have created a real or imagined space of safety. My life was split into pieces sprinkled with moments of terror and sweet remnants of comfort and grace. Nobody begins life expecting to experience what we did but evil changes everything.

This story is mine, but not all mine. The little ones who share the horror are with me, and together, we will tell our stories.

Introduction

The following is a journey of discovery, hellish memory, hope, and healing. We live with who we were created to be, multiple. We are one body and many selves. Throughout the past few years my curiosity about myself, my *parts*, and the nature of traumatic experience in childhood has led me to a Ph.D. program, a successful public speaking career, authorship, and deeper relationships. I don't know everything there is to know about dissociative identity disorder, it remains controversial and often left in the margins of psychology textbooks, but I do know my experience and I am willing to share.

I began writing this book with the intention of telling our story. It quickly became evident that multiple parts, each with their own tone, personality, and memories did not make for a cohesive narrative. Instead, this is a chronological telling, with me as the narrator. The following pages are filled with memories, journal entries, and interaction with our remarkable therapist.

For some of you, this book may be very troubling, and I suggest you have a mental health therapist to talk things over. For others, this book may reflect a life you are currently living, and still for some this is just an interesting topic and you're here to dive into unknown territory. Whatever the reason and whatever your circumstance we thank you for reading our story.

Chapter 1

"Family business is family business." Thirty years later, *His* voice still echoes in my head. Telling is a sin beyond all others but nothing will ever be okay unless we shed our skin and bare our souls. Over time, secrets fester and grow until they burst. They are rotten. They twitch and crawl inside us and we can wait no longer. In my mind, *He* is still a middle-aged man with a round belly, black curly hair, and crooked yellow teeth. Despite *his* mediocre looks, *He* is still smart, charming, and strong. I wonder what *he* is doing right now. Likely *He* is settling into a large reclining chair, lighting a cigarette, and getting ready to watch a daily dose of porn.

Discovery

My journey of discovery began about ten years ago as an undergraduate earning a degree in social work. I had just come through a long and drawn-out divorce and decided to attend a religious conference for women. The event took place over a very cold weekend in February and, to make it more fun, it was located in Northern Michigan. As one who grew up here in Michigan, I am no virgin to harsh, cold winters, but this weekend was particularly treacherous as the air warmed, then it rained, and then we were plunged into a deep freeze. The roads and walking paths were sheets of ice. A pair of ice-skates would have served me better than boots that weekend.

The trip was planned only two weeks in advance but still several other women from my tiny little church made the journey, not all of them particularly fond of the weather or my early-morning routine. Nine women had packed themselves into a chalet on a wooded hillside. It was a short, terrifying, and often comical walk to the main buildings as we would form groups of three or four to steady ourselves along the icy road. Our plans of safety were often misguided when one would lose footing and take down the entire group with a swift smack to the ass and subsequent laughter. The chalet had six sets of bunk beds. The mattresses were better suited for small limber bones, not the robust and creaky women who practiced patience only through much-needed adequate sleep. Nevertheless, we settled in for the three-day retreat.

My motivation for going on this trip was to simply have a weekend away. I had spent more than two years trying to put my marriage back together but in the end, I had come to grips with the inevitable. It was quite possibly the hardest and most liberating time of my life.

My children were just finishing elementary school. I found single motherhood to be exactly what it was before the divorce but now I didn't have to clear my actions or decisions with anyone. I got to say and do and be whomever I chose, and the consequences were mine, too. My kids were, and are, completely amazing people. I am proud of the mighty humans they have become and the way they have blown through so many hurts and challenges is inspiring. That being said, at the time of the retreat, they were young, and I was tired. I wanted a small break and this weekend was just for me.

The weekend was packed with activities from tubing down an enormous hill and sliding out onto a frozen lake, playing ping pong with my best friend in the rec room, to sipping hot chocolate by the community fireplace and talking God-things until the last of us were tired and called it a night. I wasn't one for staying up too late. My internal clock had me up before the sun. It's still that way as I have now been up for several hours and it's only 11:00 a.m.

I found out the Friday we arrived at the retreat center that the theme of the weekend was human trafficking. I was half-way through my degree in social work and I had heard the term human trafficking a few times, but it held no interest for me. While I did belong to a pretty fundamentalist Baptist church, I had absolutely no desire to be a missionary. Growing up in this kind of church I often wondered if girls were ever encouraged to do anything else.

That weekend there was a missionary who had come to teach us all about the insanity of human trafficking and what it looked like around the world. Saturday was a full day of breakout sessions, lunch, more sessions, dinner, and then free time. That was also the day the missionary gave her full presentation but I decided not to go. Instead, I headed over to a class on how to recover from a divorce, complete with how long I should wait until dating (never would be the appropriate answer here. Not their words but mine.). When I got to the class, I had placed my things on a chair and sat down. Something was nagging at me though. The instructor began talking and I needed to go, though I didn't know why, I just did. I picked up my things and headed to the other side of the building. I walked into the main auditorium and found my friend sitting in the center of the rows of chairs. I set my stuff down and expected a lecture on how slaves are being used to make our shoes and mine diamonds and work in brick factories, all overseas of course.

The missionary was talking about an incident that happened in North Carolina. Where a little girl riding a bus was groped and molested on her way home from school. The incidents continued to happen as the perpetrator was a school mate and only nine-years old, not much older than the girl. She never told anyone, and the molestation stopped after that year, but it had set into motion a lifetime of risky behavior, attention seeking, and eventually she found herself in the grips of a man who sold her to other men on what she called "dates." She was not yet a legal adult, but beyond the age of consent in her state, and began recruiting friends and co-workers to make some quick cash. She was a "bottom," which is what a pimp calls his most trusted commodity. The "bottom" is usually trusted to go out, do the recruiting, and come back.

I sat and listened to this woman's story and while I do not remember the details, I knew she was speaking things I already knew. Things that I had stuffed down. Things I had forgotten to remember. Things I never wanted to look at or say out loud. I knew in those moments that human trafficking wasn't simply an 'over there' kind of thing but happened in this country. An awakening occurred. Something sinister and dark lurked around in my past and that weekend sparked memories I could no longer ignore.

As a self-professed nerd, it was no surprise that the year following the retreat I became obsessed with everything on the topic of human trafficking. I spent hours looking up data and literature related to the subject. My new passion drove my classmates crazy. Every paper I wrote – human trafficking. Every conversation with friends – human trafficking. I became quick friends with the woman who organized the weekend retreat and she got me rolling with creating a presentation on the topic of - you guessed it - human trafficking.

A year after my revelation I didn't quite know how to channel my energy, so I talked to a few friends and we decided to open a nonprofit organization, one that would help girls who had been sexually abused and in the foster care system. Through research I found the interconnecting pieces of human trafficking involved the foster care system and early childhood trauma, two things in which I had been intimately familiar.

My friends and I began the small nonprofit and hoped for the best. The first goal included raising a lot of money, buying land, and building a massive house. I put together presentations, organized fundraisers, and joined every networking group I could find. My presentations were simple, the basics of human trafficking and my story.

By our third year in the nonprofit I had gotten pretty good at providing the education piece of presentations, but something began to change. Our second major fundraising event had more than 300 people in attendance. The banquet center was grand and beautiful. We were doing amazing work and people got behind us.

Chapter 2

The Fundraiser

I felt important as I stepped through the massive archway of the banquet center. I had somehow fooled or tricked my way in here. *I didn't belong*. This wasn't my life. It was not the life I knew, but I liked it. I could get used to such luxuries and politeness. The decorative walls, gleaming chandeliers, and woven carpets beckoned me in, and I thought, *what an incredible night this would be*.

My team met me there and the work began. We set up flowers on each table with precision and care. I began plugging in the mess of wires for speakers, projectors, microphones, and a computer. There was so much to do I didn't have time to think about what was to come. People began to pour in, people I knew and loved and who loved me.

The program lasted two hours and included dinner. I never tasted the food. I spent the evening moving from table to table and person to person to thank them for their support. My palazzo pants flowed in every direction. I felt as though I was wearing a long ball gown at a ceremonial dance. *I was a fraud*. These people were high class. *What the heck had I done?* I would need to give them details of a dream that only God could make real. My whole life was invested in the dream, but were they? *I'm not God*. I was aware but silent about how much doubt and fear flowed in and out of my consciousness.

It was time. I gently pushed my seat back and walked to the front of the great hall. My toes were freezing cold because I don't wear shoes when I speak. I walked carefully in my knee-high dress socks as the carpet transitioned into a slick dance floor. I picked up the microphone and began to speak. The words made no sense. I saw myself floating to the other side of the room and watched as I sternly spoke about the dangers of human trafficking and how foster care made children more vulnerable to this evil. I saw the red carpet and was transported to another place. I was not sure of the time or space, it was dark, and I was young.

Snap out of it!

Back in my body, tears streamed down my face. My eyes peering at the floor, I had to get it together. *Get it together!* I straightened my back and looked up. "I'm so sorry. That doesn't usually happen." I felt the blood rush to my face. I managed to gather my thoughts and continue the speech.

Had I just told them about Him?

Sadness consumed the rest of the evening, though I was told by many people how amazing the night had gone. I wouldn't know. I wasn't fully there.

The feeling of being mentally fuzzy and out of myself had happened before but not when I was the main speaker. My whole life had been brief snippets of memory that didn't make sense: flashes of myself at eleven years old, walking naked down a hall, the sound of *his* car pulling in the driveway, and *his* silhouette at my bedroom door. A few seconds here and there made up my entire childhood.

Part of me wanted to know what all had happened and part of me said it was ridiculous to wonder; it was *dangerous* to wonder. The thought of diving in too deep would unravel my entire life, a life I now loved. I loved my career as a public speaker and author. I was educating on how to prevent and respond to human trafficking; it was an amazing life and one that did not need to be disturbed. But I *was* disturbed. I could not get the images out of my head. My body felt things that were foreign and emotions found me without provocation. I needed help.

Nightmares

That night I had a dream. I stood in a large bathroom and faced a large mirror. The wall behind my reflection pulsed as if it were breathing. In and out and in and out, ripping and opening a little wider each time. The reflection of a child stared back. She had wavy brown hair and appeared to be around ten years old. Her face was marked with scratches. Dried blood crusted under her fingernails. I was her but was young. I reached for the faucet in the shower. I ached to be washed clean.

The wall behind the mirror pulsed a few more times, waned and then opened. I glanced through the opening and saw another little girl. She was mute, thin, and extremely pale. Her long dirty, thick, black hair hung like a weight around her narrow shoulders. The girl was eleven years old but no taller than a small child of maybe six or seven. Her tiny body moved slow but graceful in a long, grey nightgown. She took my hand and the hand of another small child of perhaps four years old and led us down a dimly lit hallway with dirt floors.

As the three of us walked down the hall and opened a large door. It was a grand ballroom with black and white checkered floors. The dark burgundy walls were broken into large sections by thick black curtains that hung heavy to the floor. It was clear no one ever used that room, or at least not in a long time.Tthe floor was covered in dust. We walked in for a moment as if we were looking for someone, but the room was empty.

The next room was her room, the mute girl. The walls were blue with chunks of paint missing showing the plaster underneath. Long scratches on the wall were centered over a small tan blanket crumpled on the floor. Marked with what appeared to be blood, it laid next to a single bucket. The floor was wood, and like the rest of this hidden place, dirty.

"*He* is coming!" the four-year-old whispered.

The three of us quickly shuffled from the hallway into a deeper part of the wall. We were IN the wall. *He* was calling out, "come out, come out wherever you are." We were in trouble, me more than anybody. I had told the family secrets.

The little mute girl squeezed my hand and began moving faster but we were heading toward *his* voice. I suddenly realized that she was there for *him*. *He* kept her barely alive only to torture her, to beat her, to keep her. She was *His* and only existed to serve *him*.

I tried to scream, "NO," but nothing came out. I opened my eyes and realized I had been dreaming. *He* was not there. *He* was not calling for me. My body wouldn't move. The shape of my bedroom slowly came into view. It was just a dream.

The next morning, I decided to find a therapist, someone who could help me sort through all the things I felt and saw. I needed someone who could give me tips on how to proceed through an event without getting sad and weepy. I didn't want to be sad. It was a wasted emotion. A sign of weakness and shame. Sadness never served me well and crying was a dangerous game.

Chapter 3

Finding V

A couple of weeks after the event, I looked up local therapists. My list of qualifications included being a Christian and a woman. I searched websites and asked several friends for recommendations, with no luck. I began to remember more and more, things that scared me and I wasn't sure if wanted to go there.

I decided to look at a website that had therapists in my area and, just before Christmas, I saw a picture of a therapist, older than me and probably in her fifties. I remember thinking she looked like a very kind person. I sent her an email telling her who I was and some surfacy junk about feeling depressed and having a difficult past.

The next day I received an email that she had a full caseload but would contact me if anything opened up. I let it go. Feeling a little defeated and a little relieved, I stopped looking. If it wasn't her then

it would be nobody. There was something about her.
In mid-January I received another email from her that
a spot had opened and did I want it? I jumped at it.
The following week I met my new and current-day
therapist.

Meeting day

I drove my car into the parking lot of what I
always knew to be a doctor's office but had never
noticed the other side was a therapist space. The
office was located on one side of a big white
farmhouse, probably built when the city still had dirt
roads but now it was only appropriate as a
commercial property. I walked up the wooden steps
and swung open the large glass door only to be
greeted by another door, the original to the house
likely dated at least 100 years ago. Bells rang as I
opened the creaky wooden door. It felt like a home.

V came walking out of her office, a client
followed and then promptly exited. V was short, had
a medium build and square shoulders. Her hair was
shoulder-length and the kind of soft grey that only
few older women could pull off. She wore a long blue

crocheted sweater. She stood by the door, said hello, and gestured for me to come in. A loveseat, a couple of big chairs, two tables, and a small dresser consumed all the space in her therapy room. I chose the end of the loveseat, the side close to the door. There was another door on the other side that led to the bathroom and yet another door that led to the bigger of the two children's rooms. I could see the back yard through the floor-to-ceiling window. The open blinds provided a quick escape and I could fixate on the apple tree just on the other side.

V and I spent several weeks talking about my family, divorce, and children. Ten months later I mentioned my first snippet of a bad memory. I stuttered through it and found myself distant from the words I heard come out of my mouth, words I hadn't planned on saying.

I had been seeing V for a few months when she began to ask me why I always to referred to myself as "we" or "us" instead of "me" or "I." "It's what we've always done," I searched my brain for a more sophisticated answer. "I don't know. Maybe I'm just talking for all of us who grew up in that house with *Him*."

I hesitated for a few moments. "Don't a lot of

people do that?"

She tilted her head and softened her eyes, "perhaps."

Over the next several weeks my attention was drawn more and more to the children's sand tray room. I began getting to V's office early so I could touch the little dolls, run my fingers through the sand, and set up the little girl dolls in the large dollhouse fixed on a shelf.

Christmas was coming soon, and I had been seeing V for nearly a year. "Why don't you keep a daily journal?" V asked. "We could read it at the beginning of every session and that way, when you have something come up, we can read it and talk about it."

That sounded like a great idea to me. Most days walking into her office my mind went blank. Trying to say anything about my past left me without words. I began keeping a journal. I wrote every morning and every evening. Most entries were not very exciting but it gave us an opportunity to say what we were feeling and thinking in between sessions with V.

Chapter 4

Grandparents

My father's family's norms and expectations were in contrast to that of my mother's family. *He* was born to a mother who abandoned her husband (my grandfather), my father, and *his* siblings as a toddler. My grandfather's new wife immigrated here (from Sicily) with her mother. Great Grandma Rose was a tiny woman who spent most of her time smiling at her family and taking it all in. I remember Great Grandma Rose sitting in the corner of the kitchen while my grandmother, who eventually had four children with my grandfather, stirred a pot of fresh tomato sauce. A lit cigarette poised over the pot, she joked about the added flavor when an overgrown ash fell and became mixed in with the stewed tomatoes. Amused by her own "poots," her giggles often propelled a symphonic string of farts.

My Italian grandparent's house was always

loud. As my aunts got older, they and my grandmother would stir the pot, literally and figuratively, with family gossip and nobody was off limits. Their knack for knocking down the family opposition while serving up fresh ground sausage, homemade pasta, and tomato sauce, was almost an art form.

My second stepmother was often the topic of the day. Her frail stature, chain-smoking, and pill addiction was enough fuel to keep the family in gossip for years to come. My Italian family didn't have much to stand on, as they too kept Marlboro and Camel in business, and drank wine and whiskey while talking shit about the rest of the family.

My mother's side of the family was intent on respect, dignity, and never, never should there be a fart released in the company of others. Up to the day of my proper English grandmother's passing, she claimed she had never passed gas. I respected her claim but knew this was unlikely.

My mother's family was rooted in music and art. Between my grandmother, mother, and uncles, I experienced them play the piano, drums, and guitar. And everyone sang. My mother was usually the star of family music time and my grandmother recorded everything with pride. Family music time consisted of the same ten or so of Grandma's favorite hymns. After my mother died my grandmother taped everything I sang as well. She taught me from a very young age how to sing and play the piano.

While I do love music and continue to play and sing, my heart is poured out when I oil paint. My introduction to art and everything crafty, again, came early when visiting Grandma's house on the weekends and many days during the summer months. My grandparents frequently created plaques and toys out of wood. My grandfather, the woodworker and my grandmother, the painter. I enjoyed the precision of tole painting and how one could create a beautiful design with dots and swirls of paint, but I found a passion in the freedom of working with oils. The ability to push paint around on a canvas and make simple landscapes come alive with color and shadow continues to be part of my day.

From time to time, my father's side of the family and mother's side of the family got together. At the invitation of my grandmother on my mother's side, those times felt odd. A mixing of two worlds that would never meld.

The contrasting personalities of my mother's

family with my father's family became of no consequence when at the age of ten I was no longer permitted to talk or see either sets of grandparents. My father's parents were suddenly off limits due to them believing my sister for the horrendous abuse my father had inflicted on her. Rumors of *him* also molesting my aunts came out at this time. I was barred from contact from my mother's parents because according to my stepmother, I had become "too churchy." My interaction with my father's parents ceased immediately but over time my restricted access to my mother's parents loosened and little by little I was able to resume my weekend visits.

My church days with Grandma were an escape from everything I knew. The thought that Jesus was someone that could cure me of my persistent failings was comforting *and* shameful. *If Jesus could save me, then He has seen me, and if He has seen me, He knows how gross and unworthy I am.* According to my father and stepmother I was dirty, fat, and a liar. I needed Jesus and was grateful for His acceptance, but only as a consequence of me accepting Him. I accepted Jesus as a child. Unraveling the truth about who He was, and is, continues to confound me, yet still I believe.

According to my grandmother, it was my

responsibility above all things to honor my mother and father and in her words to "be sweet" if I wanted to be a good Christian, and I *did* want to be a good Christian. I went to school and told all my friends about Jesus. I told my father and stepmother about Jesus. While my father made it a point to use a massive Bible as a punishment, *he* was irritated by my constant fascination with a savior that was just for me.

The Bible at the end of the hall was always open and consumed the entire table. It sat beneath an old painting of a man praying over his bread and soup. It always made me hungry. "Go read it," *He* would tell me whenever *he* was bothered by my mention of church or what I had learned. I would go to the end of the hall and peer at the words, the book opened to Psalms. I couldn't read very well and certainly couldn't read the old King James version of the Bible. I pretended and that was enough. My father also used the "honor your mother and father" bit to keep me from telling the family business. My loyalty to *Him* was firmly in place but *he* was hedging *his* bets with the promise of Hell should I consider uttering the family secrets. In addition to the persistent reminder of how I was to honor *Him*, I was told that the Bible had a lot of examples of fathers and daughters in "close" relationships. "It's a culture thing, nobody here has caught on yet," *he* would remind me.

My grandmother's perfectionistic call for the appearance of being "beyond reproach" was evident in the way she refused to leave the house without applying her makeup, which called "putting on her face." Her painted nails, jewelry, shoes, and lipstick were all perfectly matched to her pencil skirt and matching suit jacket.

Words were of particular importance to her. The only time I remember her getting upset with me is when she caught me playing with army figurines and I shouted, "die sucker, die!" At six-years-old, this was a phrase I had heard from my grandfather's war movies.

"No, no, we don't say things like that," my grandmother's face contorted into someone I didn't recognize. She had never been angry with me before. I stopped playing with those army figurines and tried my best to stick with more appropriate "good girl" activities, like drawing and roller skating.

Chapter 5

Grandma

My life is full of tremendous experiences and opportunities. Looking back now, it's a miracle all the pieces of my life led to one of my greatest joys, public speaking. Being a public speaker was never on my list of things to do. When I was in high school and the career counselor asked, "what do you plan to do after graduation?" I pictured myself on stage as a singer or actress but never thought my life would lead me to the stage for education and inspirational purposes.

I began my 'on stage' career early, as one who sang and performed for crowds in plays and church cantatas. My grandmother encouraged me and pushed my talent for singing in the direction she wanted her daughter to go. For my grandmother, I *was* Kathy; the daughter she lost in the winter of 1978.

My mother's death came as a shock to the

entire family. She went into the hospital with appendicitis and never came out. A blood clot had formed in her leg and traveled to her lungs. At 21 months old, I had no idea what was happening.

A few years later, while at my grandparent's house, I found photos of my mother lying in her coffin. I stared at those photos, trying to feel something, anything, but nothing came. I wasn't sad. I wasn't missing her. I didn't remember her. I wondered how someone could have small children and still die. Nothing made sense.

My childhood was filled with different names, Screaming Mimi, Anus, Grace, Ignoramus, but my grandmother called me by my mother's name, Kathy. Every once in a while Grandma would catch herself and call me Amy but most of the time I was happy to be Kathy. Kathy was sweet, gifted, intelligent, loved God with all her heart, and could never hurt a soul. These were the things I knew of my mother, told to me by family and church members who looked at me with pity only to reminisce about sweet, perfect Kathy. Memorialized as a saint, she was everything I knew I could never be.

I don't remember my mother. The sound of her voice, the smell of her hair, and touch of her skin all faded away. I am grateful for the many cassette tapes I have of her singing, talking, laughing. I can hear her now in my daughter's voice, as she has the same sweet timbre.

I don't know that Kathy would have dreamt a life of public speaking for her little girl. Certainly, a life of submission to a husband, raising babies, and serving the Church were closer to her wish list. Her writings and actions said as much.

Performance in high school for me was something I treasured, though I rarely received a leading part due to my not being quite as 'cute' as the other girls in my class. I was taller than most, wider than most, louder than most, and as one professor later stated, had "a very interesting voice."

I have come to appreciate my time on stage. The privilege of having a grandmother who paid for voice lessons and encouraged me to sing in front of people became an integral part of who I am today. I was a performer from a young age and a performer I remain.

My desire to do something in the areas of human trafficking and trauma was more than I understood at the time, but I could not set it aside. I had an internal need to do something that was far beyond myself and to bring awareness and hope. My purpose is not to convince anyone that evil exists, I'm here to help those who have come into intimate contact with its presence.

As a little girl I dreamt of days when I would get to see my grandparents. Grandma usually picked me up and took me to McDonald's' for chicken nuggets and an orange pop. Once at her house I usually headed upstairs to the craft room. The other bedroom was my room. Sporting an oversized button-down shirt, the both of us would get to work. Her words were always encouraging even if my paint had all run together turning into dirty brown blobs on a canvas.

Her craft room was stacked high with empty pill bottles and worn-out plastic butter dishes that were filled with trinkets and orphaned screws and nails. Grandma grew up in the midst of the Great Depression and her home reflected an obsession with preserving and keeping everything that she thought practical for current or future use. For me, her house was full of wonder. She had an imagination for items for which they were not created and that made my mind race with ideas. Once at home, *He* had stored up bits and pieces of lumber in the garage, and with a little ingenuity, I came up with ways to turn a skateboard into a scooter and nail together lopsided shelving units.

I loved being at my grandparent's house. It was free from yelling and chores. Grandpa thought himself a funny Irish magic man and convinced me he could do things with his mind. I was fascinated with his abilities and often tried to make objects appear or move by staring at them. Standing at the side door he would proclaim, "OPEN SASAME!" The garage door at the far end of the driveway would begin to open. Eyes wide and mouth agape, he got me every time. It wasn't until I was twelve years old that I figured out the button for the garage was on the wall next to the door. It was too high for me to see it. He was a fun grandpa. He passed when I was seventeen years old and I regret not getting to know him better. I think he was a good man and there aren't many of those around.

My grandparent's back yard sloped down from the house and about halfway back there was a great big cherry tree. Hanging from a sturdy branch was a tire swing. For a couple of weeks, the smell of cherry blossoms was absolute heaven. The shade from the tree provided the perfect protection from the sun. Grabbing the sides of the tire that hung from that cherry tree I would back up as far as I could and then in one fluid motion throw my legs into the center of the tire. I leaned back and peered straight through the branches into the sky. Time vanished.

Sundays were reserved for church. Just in case, something was missed in the morning sermon, we went again in the evening. Grandma played piano in the evenings. Throughout the weekend she quoted bible verses and reminded that ladies don't shout or sit cross-legged while wearing a dress. Most of the women in the church wore long-sleeved dresses that cinched at the waste and dropped to the floor. Grandma put them to shame with her brightly colored suit jacket and matching pencil skirt. Bright red, blue, purple, yellow, or green, Grandma never left the house 'undone.' In the morning, she would emerge like a model from the pages of Good Housekeeping magazine. She tried her best to teach me to be a lady; it didn't stick.

Heading back home on Sunday nights were difficult, for me as well as for Grandma. After a dinner of popcorn, apples, and cheese while we cuddled on the bed watching her favorite mystery show, Grandma and Grandpa would take me home. The sun had usually disappeared by the time I arrived. Before getting out of the car, Grandma would look at me and say, "be sweet and don't forget to honor your mother and your father." There it was. The verse that would keep me swirling in a dichotomy of loyalty to God and loyalty to *Him* for years.

Chapter 6

Our Story

Christmas always brought out the traditionalist in me and I found myself rifling through many of my grandmother's pictures and audio tapes. She recorded everything she could. She prided herself on being the church and family historian. I sat on the floor and carefully pulled out photo album after photo album from Grandpa's old army footlocker. Grandpa had lugged that footlocker all over Germany during World War II. He never talked about the war but I could tell he was proud of his time in the service.

I was excited to show V the treasures I had found at our next visit.

Settling into the loveseat in V's office, I said, "I found some tapes and put them on my phone. Do you want to listen?"

"Yes, of course," V said.

I pulled out my phone and pressed *play*. My grandmother's voice was engaging and repeatedly asked, "Amy, you wanna sing Jesus loves me?" My three-year-old voice emerged over the sound of toys clanking in the background, "hello?" I said as if answering Mickey Mouse on the toy telephone.

"Come on, sing Jesus loves me," Grandma prodded a little harder.

In my three-year-old determination, I stated, "Jesus don't love me."

"Jesus DON'T love me! Fodder say NO! He DON'T love me! He FIND me and BREAK me!"

The sounds of the toy telephone continued as I stopped the recording. Astonished at what we had just heard, V asks me to play it again. We listened to it a few more times and each time, I felt more and more validated about the feelings and flashbacks I have had my entire life. Listening to my little voice I knew more than ever, it was *His* intention to break me, to break all of us, from the very beginning. We didn't yet know how horrendous *he* had been.

I was determined to know and understand more, to fill in the gaps, but I couldn't do it alone. I needed V and she needed the other little ones to tell their stories.

V put her arm around me, I leaned into her, and wept. Her hands draped over my head, keeping the chaos and darkness from toppling out onto the floor.

"Hey, Amy?" V sat up and focused intently on the recording.

"Yeah?"

"You said there were a lot of kids in the house, why not bring in pictures and we can make kind of like a little family diagram?"

"I can do that!" My thoughts immediately went to the footlocker where many of our family photos had been stored.

"It's kinda of weird though. There were so many of us kids that came and went. I'll bring a bunch next time." I straightened myself and felt tall

and accomplished. We were really going to dig into
the family secrets (a big fat no-no, but it was also
intriguing).

Over the next couple of weeks, V and I placed
each little girl around on a posterboard. We labeled
each of them with their names and ages. Mimi is four
years old. Six is six years old. Eight is, you guessed
it, eight years old. Anna is ten years old. Iggy is
eleven years old. There were also pictures of me from
toddler to adulthood. A current picture of me was set
in the middle of the diagram.

Chapter 7

Morning Walk

As I slip on the snug red-plaid harness over Sully's neck, he looks a bit like a fancy lumberjack's pup, instead of belonging to a middle-aged woman. I've been exercising off and on for decades and dieting off and on for the same stretch of torturous time, yet here I remain, the same size 16, the same round cheeks, bad hips, and wonky toe (that's what I call the toe next to the big one, the one that has crept its way to the right in a crooked jag, complete with an erect knuckle). It all hurts like hell.

Every morning I take a hot bath to loosen my back and hips and vigorously massage the wonkified toe. The foot beating doesn't seem to work but the rhythm of it makes me feel somehow accomplished and ready for another two-mile walk. It stormed last night and the grass is bright from the much-needed rain after a short, hot drought left all of Southern Michigan looking like a prickly desert.

Yesterday's storms brought a cool breeze and plenty of rain. As long as there is some moisture, the grass here never really dies. It's amazing to me how tough nature can be. Even in the winter the grass remains green. I suppose everything God has created is built for some level of resilience.

This day started out as a day of emptiness. I woke up with little on my mind. My business is going pretty well, the kids are doing their own thing and hopefully enjoying their morning, but eh, it is of no consequence to me this morning.

Walking Sully on a leash that stretches for several feet beyond a reasonable grasp, I have to be careful because if let go he would be gone like a flash with a built-in twenty-foot head start. Lord, he does like to run. His one blue eye is the only indication of a Husky breed. He has white fur that goes on for miles and one floppy brown ear makes him the cutest mutt on the planet, or at least in this neighborhood. The dogs around here are chunky, not lean like Sully, and all mixed with some sort of Beagle. I have never understood the attraction to wiry hair and incessant barking. They seem to represent their owners - grumpy and stout.

With the dog's leash in my hand, I put on

tennis shoes and headed out the door. I flung my cross-body bag around my neck. They are perfect for carrying the essentials: water, poop bags, my phone, and a few note cards and pens. Time outdoors is my time to listen to an audiobook. There is nothing better than walking in step with the rhythm of the speaker's voice. I like to choose books where the author is also the narrator. They know their shit and don't stumble around trying to make sentences they didn't compose come together. This day's organized retreat is the same as any other except for the storm that came through the previous day.

The storm had actually begun two days ago with crashes of thunder and lightning stretching on through the night and into the next day. A drop in temperature from the 90s to the low- 40s is a welcome break. We are not used to that kind of heat and for the past few weeks it has been hot. I am looking forward to this morning's walk. I don't always. Some days I want to lie around in my pajamas and drink coffee but my morning walk has become a ritual and my head is not right without it.

For the first mile Sully is so excited, smelling and pissing on rocks, trees, and weeds along the way. I suppose this has become his ritual as well. We trot down our quiet little street. Not many people are out this early. Two more hours and every Beagle-bred dog with his owner will be meandering from house to house looking for a gal to chat up. *Dirty old men, that's all they are, dirty old men.* Ten years we have lived here and every summer another dirty old man enters the community, stopping to chat about the weather, calling me "beautiful" and asking why I don't marry already. *Must be a lesbian*, they're probably thinking, because of course, every middle-aged single woman must be a lesbian. Maybe it's a rule but then again, I've never followed the rules. *Screw 'em. I got Sully.*

Me and the goofy-eyed pup round the corner and climb up a small hill. The landscape changes as the sidewalk on the outskirts of the subdivision now borders a main road. On our left, a row of trees and backyards and on the right, zooming cars and corn fields. Sully darts from tree to tree to rock to tree, marking every spot until he is empty, though that does not stop him from trying. By the time we reach this stretch of the path, he lifts his leg with nary a whistle of piss left in him. *Such a neurotic dog.* Our sidewalk ends and we pass through a field of grass until we reach the edge of town. Our steps take us behind the corner gas station where the attendants watch and wave to us from the window. We walk beyond the gas pumps and find the sidewalk again; Sully resumes his neuroticism once more.

The smells of the small-town transition as we walk from the fields of dandelions and sweet corn to the gas station and carwash. The smell of diesel gasoline and murky water overwhelms the fragrance of nature. It's not long and we again have homes to the left and the busy main road to the right. I look forward to the same cars in the morning as people politely wave as they drive. I believe Sully and I have become the quirky town characters in someone else's smalltown play.

We are known by the locals. I hope I didn't wear my white panties under my black leggings again, but then again, we're already odd, no one would think of us any differently. Perhaps it isn't the underwear that neighbors noticed but rather the half-dried worms I can't seem to leave all alone and abandoned on the sunny pavement. A light rain or a dewy morning brings the worms to the surface, and I can't help but think they got lost. Poor little things, no eyes, no ears, no brain to speak of, I can't help but feel a kindness toward them. They are simple creatures, and shouldn't we all take care of the simpler ones here on earth? Days like today, I stop every few steps, bend over, gently pinching the worm between my thumb and forefinger, and sling him to the grass. Bending over I usually smack Sully in the head with my bag, assuming the closeness will result in a pet and a praise. He's so naïve.

Our morning journey takes us beside one the most beautiful homes in town. It's a three-story white colonial and hidden behind trees, bushes, and an array of flowering shrubs. Every morning the landscape is a little different; flowers bloom and wither as others emerge under the dark green foliage. A kaleidoscope of nature and tradition move together. Here is where my favorite trees hang their heavy branches. They are not huge trees, but full, rich, and sporting tiny little red beads. This morning I find most of the red beads have given way to the storm and are now scattered across the grass, sidewalk, and street; *storms change things*. I can't help but think of Mimi and her storm.

Chapter 8

Four-years-old

My second year began with the death of my
mother. After my mother's passing, I immediately
went to live with my grandparents. Under much
protest, they returned me to *Him* the following
Spring, just after my third birthday. At that time, *he*
had already moved into a bigger house and married
my mother's best friend. I don't remember the look of
her face as much as much as I remember her short
stubby fingers and bitten fingernails. My grandmother
always had manicured, long, painted fingernails. Her
long fingers suited her piano-playing. She often put
my small hands on hers when she played. I would run
my finger along her smooth fingernails like it was a
velvet painting.

The new stepmother was no replacement for
my grandmother. She had four boys and a girl and I
was still the youngest. My half-sister was seven years
older than me. It was difficult to keep track of how
many kids and adults lived at our house. We always

had a new cousin who was pregnant move in, and
then a baby appeared. Or a whole family that was
some distant relative or friend would show up with an
RV and no money. My father was the never-ending
savior for the 'down-on-your-luck' cohort.

The new house was a large red brick mid-
century colonial. Upstairs had four bedrooms, two on
either side of the big bathroom in the center of the
hall, to the left was mine and the boys' room and to
the right, *His* and the stepmother's room. My sisters
shared a room at the end of the hall, the oldest boy
had a room to himself at the other end. The hall closet
door was directly across from my bedroom door.
Beyond all of the winter coats in the hall closet there
was a small door that led to the attic.

The girls didn't bother with me much, I was
younger and had little to offer as a playmate. I had the
'honor' of sharing a room with the three youngest
boys. They were typical redneck suburbanites,
dressed in dirty jeans and tight off-white tank tops. I
was tall for my age and met eye-to-eye with the
youngest boys.

I can still see the peach-colored walls and the
bunk beds jammed in from end to end. The window
was up so high all I could ever see was sky; my best

daydreaming came from that window. There was no space for toys in the tiny bedroom. All games and toys were in the terrifying basement!

The outside of the house was nice. It had matured trees to climb. The neighborhood was a large suburb of Detroit and well-maintained. I remember winding streets and nearly jumping curbs as I drove, or pretended to drive, our brown-paneled station wagon. *He* and I often went for car rides.

I had on little cotton shorts, thin ones that were more like pajama bottoms. I didn't quite care about how fashionable they were, I was pleased to find clean clothes from day to day. *He'd* call to me and ask if I wanted to go for a ride. The answer was always and excited "YES!"

We had a long brown and tan striped station wagon with tan leather seats. The front seat went all the way across and as the only passenger, I got to sit in the front. The sticky leather seats skidded across the back of my thighs like wet hot tar being pulled from a roof. I tried to pull my shorts further down my legs but it was useless and honestly it just made me frustrated. Though the sun heated the seats so much they practically fused to my skin, this was a much better position than the rear-facing 'far-back' seat, where every acceleration resulted in being thrust face-first into the big window. I imagine there were many people in cars behind us who got a kick out of my dad intentionally giving the gas pedal a good stomp, only to see us thrown around the back end of the car.

Climbing into the car in the summer was always a process of cooling off my legs as I went, the leather practically setting fire to anything that touched it. But no matter, a solo ride with *Him* always meant I got to drive! Or, at least, I thought I was driving.

With one move, *He* lifted me, separated my legs so they dangled off to the sides of *his*, set me down, and placed my hands on the steering wheel.

"It's all you now. Steer straight, so we don't crash," *He'd* say.

I was *His* traveling buddy, and usually the first volunteer to run errands. Sitting on *his* lap, it was my job to steer the car. I was so intent on receiving high praise for not crashing that I did my best to ignore the pressure between my legs. My compliance made *Him* happy and I ached for *his* approval. Car rides continued for several more years.

Chapter 9

Doctor

Friends were difficult to find and keep but with nine children in the house there was always activity. When I was four-years old I asked my stepmother if she could make my stepbrothers play with me. She yelled upstairs for them to play with me. All four boys, ages five, eight, ten, and thirteen, met me at the top of the stairs. The oldest boy smirked and uncharacteristically put up no resistance. I was eager to play the game we often played together - Doctor.

The oldest boy told me to go into my bedroom. He said, "lay down and I'll get your medicine." The youngest and oldest boy went into the bathroom, whispers and giggles crept around the corner. The other two pulled my shirt up and said, "is this where it hurts?" They ran their fingers along my torso, pretending to perform surgery. This was the usual way doctor was played. The boy's disappearance into the bathroom made me suspicious. Suddenly shy and mute, I began to sink into the bottom bunk. The two older boys returned from the bathroom with a cup of "medicine" and told me to drink it. I took the thick green plastic cup and took a drink. My throat stung. The boys laughed hysterically. I had just swallow fresh urine. I pushed the cup back to the boys and the oldest said "no, you have to drink it." The three younger boys held my arms and legs while the oldest put the cup to my lips and poured. I never asked to play with them again.

Chapter 10

Fire

There were many hot days in the Summer of 1980. It was also the summer of the massive two-day storm; the sky turned puke green and the threat of tornados loomed for two full days. I imagine a pretty scary, or maybe fascinating, sight for those who lived through it.

The boys and I had been playing in the neighborhood, collecting little orange beady things from the trees and throwing them at each other. We ran from house to house searching for friends to join in the fun. Across the street there were a set of twins my age. Brigette and Bradly. They were quiet and there was something wrong with Bradly, his head always bounced from one side to the other. I never said anything about it but my staring must have been obvious to his mother who always told me, "Everyone is different" and "be kind."

I was as kind as I could be but still found myself fascinated with how his head seemed to exist on a thin hinge. *It going to roll right off if he keeps doing that*, I thought. Brigette and Bradly's mother was kind, especially to me. She often made sandwiches and brought out peanut butter crackers. That hot day in summer they were not home and all my options for gathering food or drink from the neighbors had run out. I had to go home. It was mid-afternoon and I began to bend over and winced in pain from the pinching in my stomach.

It was a very hot summer day and I had been outside since the sun came up. It was typical for us to not have breakfast or lunch, but I was thirsty and got tired of sneaking water from the neighbor's hose. Kool-Aid sounded good and I thought I might be able to grab a hotdog bun or something to stop my stomach from growling.

I had watched the stepbrothers all go inside a few minutes before and thought maybe they had gathered some food. *They better not have grabbed it all*. I rushed into the house and *HE* had been standing near the door. I didn't make it past the foyer. *He* grabbed my arm and led me to the half-wall that separated the living room from the hallway. The boys were lined up from oldest to youngest, their pants on the floor. I knew what to do but I resisted. I dug my little feet into the floor and made *him* drag me. I didn't understand why I was in trouble, not that a reason would have mattered. My crying always infuriated *Him* and with one swift move my face hit the wall.

"Put your hands up!" *He* snapped. Taking the usual position, feet squared and chest out, *he* kept at it, "Who did it? Who started the fire?"

I immediately knew I didn't do it. I hadn't even heard about a fire. This was a gross miscarriage of justice and I began screaming, first quietly, then louder, and louder as I slowly backed away from the wall. "I didn't do it. I didn't do it. I DIDN'T DO IT."

Hoping *he* would have mercy and let me retrieve the Kool-Aid and hotdog bun I so desperately wanted, I was back at the wall, shorts and underwear yanked to the floor and wrists held tight. *He* took off *his* belt and I thought *he* was coming for me first. I shrank and braced for impact but *he* didn't break with *his* usual routine and started beating the oldest boy first.

I didn't look but heard the boys count faintly

as the belt swung. Mine was coming. I dropped my head on the wall and tried to scrape a clump of dirt off my big toe. One by one the boys got theirs, counting through their crying and then silence, crying and then silence, crying and then silence, until finally *he* was behind me. I heard the belt slide through the air and then…..then, burning, stinging, so much pain! *He* had spanked me before, and often, but my defiance made *him* unusually angry. *He* got a few swipes in before I threw myself on the floor and crawled into a corner. Soaked with urine, my feet slipped, trying with everything I had in me to disappear into the wall, *get smaller …...be invisible.* New hot welts grew as I disappeared into the wall. My father yelled, "clean your shit up and go to your room." Mimi and I promptly obeyed.

Chapter 11

Mimi

"Tell me about Mimi," V said.

"Well, I don't know a ton. She was little like me but tall for a four-year-old. She looked like one of those American Girl Dolls. She has big icy blue eyes. She always seemed a little sad, sometimes super mad, but mostly just wanted a mom."

I looked down at her picture and picked it up. "She loved this dress."

Mimi's picture was her at her fifth birthday, wearing a red and white cowgirl outfit. The hat, also red with white candy stripes along the rim, dangled from her neck.

"She looks so sad here," V said.

"Yeah, I wasn't there, I don't know why she would have been sad, but she did scream a lot and that got her in trouble, so maybe that's it. That's how she got her name, Screaming Mimi." I looked at the picture again and said, "She's really whiny. Ya know?"

V glanced at me and then crinkled her forehead. "Well, she is only four. Screaming Mimi sounds kind of mean. I hope she's okay with me just calling her Mimi."

I nodded in agreement. I wasn't going to convince V that Mimi was anything but an angel. I left it alone and set the picture back on the diagram next to the picture of Six.

"I was thinking about her the other day after that big storm we had."

"That sounds interesting, tell me more." V turned toward me a little more and pulled out her notepad to write down any interesting tidbits.

Chapter 12

Mimi's Storm

I remember hearing about it mostly, but Mimi got lost for a whole day. Mimi left early in the morning and had lost track of time. We all shared a Big Wheel and that morning Mimi thought she would get up really early and ride it before anybody else got the chance to claim it. It was a really windy morning and had rained all night. The rain cleared but the wind made it difficult to steer the Big Wheel on the sidewalk. Mimi decided to head to the catwalks with the Big Wheel. The best one was near our elementary school. It was in the middle of a large field with massive power lines running through it. But it also went downhill for about half of a mile, perfect for battling the wind.

Mimi spent all day playing in the catwalks and running in between the monstrous electricity pylons. She collected rocks and put them in her pockets. She pretended that the whole field was her friend and the pylons talked to each other.

"She's our Queen," Mimi's imagination had one pylon speaking to the others.

"I'm not your Queen," Mimi raised her arms, "I'm a Princess."

Mimi's play and Big Wheel adventures stretched on for several hours. The sky began to get darker and darker, and the wind picked up speed. Mimi started to get a little scared and inadvertently left the Big Wheel behind as she began to run home.

Mimi ran across and down streets she didn't recognize. It was late afternoon and she realized she didn't know how to get home. She looked up and saw the sky churning and swirling. The trees bent, almost touching the ground. Mimi was lost.....again. In reality, she was only a few houses from her home. Looking around for some sign of which way to start walking, or running, as the rain started to beat down on her little head, a frantic woman came running from a garage and pulled Mimi inside. Mimi was not afraid, the stranger seemed familiar somehow. The woman was tall and lanky with long, stringy, brown hair. She took Mimi into the house. They watched the

storm together behind a large bay window. The sky

spun and screamed as it tore apart the little beady trees, the ones with the little orange pellets.

Mimi watched the neighborhood transformed the perfectly manicured yards into landing strips for falling branches, leaves, and even some roof shingles. Mimi's thoughts turned to the trouble she knew was coming…..when, or if, she made it home. Getting lost was nothing new and she was accustomed to neighbors bringing her home. One would think she would learn not to wander too far.

With her hand on the windowsill Mimi felt the lady standing behind her. A gentle weight covered her shoulders as the neighbor draped a towel over Mimi. Her little hands grabbed the edge of the towel and drew it to her chin. The trees outside bent in half and green clouds continued their dance. Fascinated with the storm, for a few moments, Mimi forgot about her life at home. With one hand rested on Mimi's shoulder, the neighbor lady bent down and handed Mimi a sandwich.

"Oh, thanks." Confused, Mimi looked down. "But I'm not supposed to."

"Not supposed to what, sweetheart?"

"Eat," Mimi blurted out matter-of-factly.

The lady's eyes widened, "What do you mean?" Mimi looked at the peanut butter and jelly in Mimi's hand. "It's okay to eat here. I won't tell. I promise."

Mimi met eyes with the lady and took a bite of the sandwich. Every bite filled her up, not only with food, but with shame. Her gaze turned again to the storm outside. She could tell it had been a little while since she had been gone as her shorts were almost dry. Every passing minute made her more afraid of what awaited her.

The branches on the trees lengthened toward the sky. The leaves settled into a heavy drooping position. The rain and wind were gone. The lady told Mimi it's time to go, "come on, your house is this way." The lady took Mimi's hand and led her outside. The wet pavement glowed with a bright pink hue from the setting sun. Not wanting to walk on the sidewalk and be swallowed up by the novel shades, Mimi's tiny wet toes sloshed through puddles as she walked on the grass.

The walk home seemed long. It was only took a few minutes to walk but for Mimi, it was an eternity. Mimi recognized the giant maple tree that stood in the center of her yard. The storm didn't hurt the tree at all, it was as big and strong as ever. The long branches stretched out toward the house, inviting her home. Every step up the driveway was heavy. The neighbor let go of Mimi's little fingers and waved her on.

The door opened long before Mimi reached the porch. She took a few more steps and the door closed. Mimi felt a hand on her back and then she was pushed into the half-wall. Before *He* could unbuckle *his* belt, she began to cry and scream in a shrill voice, "I didn't mean to! I didn't mean to!"

Moving faster, *He* lifted her to *his* face and screamed, "YOU NEVER MEAN TO!"

Mimi froze. *He* was unmoved. Her persistent whining made *him* angrier, swinging the belt at her little body until there is no more to give for either of them. Her screeching cries became faint and worn, and *he* lost the motivation to keep going. *He* left Mimi alone on the floor. Her shorts were around her ankles, wet again and reeked with urine. Mimi's will and energy were gone. That was the game, *his* game, *his* rules, and she never won.

Chapter 13

Half-walls

Mimi walked by the half-wall every day, all day. The front door foyer was occupied by a constant pile of mismatched shoes that acted as a doorstop for anyone who swung the door open too fast. To *Him*, this was a disgrace. The house was to be immaculate at all times. This was an impossibility for the nearly dozen residents. Mimi hates the cluster of shoes and sees no use for such painful confinement. Even in the coldest weather, Mimi muttered, "I HATE shoes!"

Mimi's growing feet never quite fit the shoes she was given, and she did everything to not wear the stupid things. The staircase was to the left of the foyer and the living room was to the right. A long hall stretched from the front door to the kitchen and on the way, there were two half-walls framing the entrance into the living room. The half-walls created a narrow path led into the living room, where the couch and tv were situated. None of the kids were allowed into that room anyway, at least not without invitation. Even

then, Mimi and the others were designated to sit on
the floor. Mimi thought it was gross, *I don't want to
sit on that nasty booger carpet, no way*. She doesn't
dare say things like that out loud, *He* will hear, *he*
hears everything!

The stark walls were not decorated with
paintings or any color but marked with streaks of
ketchup, dirt, a little blood, and a multitude of varying
sized fingerprints. The half-walls were at the center of
the house, you can't get to the kitchen which was
straight ahead, or the formal dining room, two steps
down to the left of the kitchen, without first passing
the half-walls. There's a half-bath situated between
the kitchen and dining room. The smell of urine
lingered in the doorway because the boys didn't care
to aim straight.

The kitchen was unusually small but the
corner cupboard was big enough for Mimi to hide.
This was another room that was off-limits until chores
needed to be done or we were called in to eat. Mimi
had a knack for stealing food and was closely
monitored by whatever adult happened to be there at
the time.

Across from the bathroom was the basement
door and it was usually closed. Mimi only went down

there to play with the few toys that were in the house. Trying her best not to alert anyone she crept down the wood steps, one by one, as slow as she could.

The formal dining room also had a large door-wall that led to the back yard. To Mimi it was expansive but really, the yard was only the size of a typical city lot in the suburbs of Detroit. It still held magic in its trees and Mimi longed to spend her days outside.

The formal dining room was not used for much except meals. It had a massive wood table with twelve high-back chairs. They seemed royal, with their delicate carvings and layers of shiny lacquer. The chairs towered above Mimi's head. There was an expansive red-brick fireplace that spanned the length of the back wall. Mimi spent hours pretending the concrete hearth was a dance floor, and she, the resident ballerina. Mimi hummed softly as she twirled on tiptoes from one side to the next, dreaming of pale pink leotards and perfectly fitting ballet slippers.

Most days the boys tromped through the house without regard for knocking down little Mimi, but she *ain't no wimp*. She was tall for a four-year-old, and muscly for a little girl, no doubt obtained by climbing trees. Her shoulder-length, brown hair was thick and wavy. Most days it was so knotted up that no comb can get through it. Her big, blue eyes, and simple, coy smile made her endearing to many adults. Mimi was special. Regardless of how many kids were in the house, Mimi was always the youngest, *perfect for pushing around and blaming everything on*, she often thought.

Chapter 14

Butter and Syrup

Punishment at the pole wasn't much different than the wall, other than it was a solitary event with no witnesses or additional participants. The boys weren't down there, not like Mimi. She always seems to be in trouble, screaming, running through the house, or leaving the door open. The options for 'in trouble' were endless.

One Sunday afternoon was particularly troublesome for Mimi. So hungry, she gripped her stomach tight, sharp pain radiated through her body and it was getting the best of her. "Be quiet, be sweet, don't see me," Mimi whispered to herself.

He and Stepmom had been gone a long time and usually that meant they would be returning with groceries. There was still no guarantee of getting food once they returned. Mimi was often the last one fed and *He* and Stepmom restricted food for all the kids.

Stepmom often told Mimi that she was too fat and could skip a meal or two.

Mimi saw the car pull in the driveway and quickly moved away from the front window. Moving as quick as she could, she ran to the kitchen and hid under the table. The door opened and she heard *Him* mumbling something to Stepmom. The heavy grocery bags forced them into a rhythm as they walked down the hall and into the kitchen. Mimi's eyes lit up when they placed four large brown paper bags on the kitchen table. Crouching down under the table, Mimi's chubby fingers gripped the wooden spindle in anticipation. Knowing she might get caught, Mimi waited for the sound of footsteps to move away down the hall back toward the door. As quick as she could, Mimi slid out from under the table and reached into one of the paper bags. She pulled out a stick of butter. Going back in for something else, she pulled out a bottle of maple syrup.

The footsteps returned. Mimi shrunk back under the table. She fumbled with the butter wrapper and opened the top to the syrup. Biting into the butter, she gagged, it had already started to melt from the summer heat. She then put the bottle of syrup to her lips and drank. Like a soothing elixir, the syrup slid down her throat. A smile stretched across Mimi's face as the sweetness of the syrup eased the pain of hunger. Mimi let out sighs of contentment.

Just beyond the table legs, Mimi caught sight of *His* shoes pointed in her direction. As if in slow motion, *his* face appeared in front of Mimi. Reaching for *his* rebellious daughter, *his* massive hand grabbed her upper arm and slid her across the floor. Still gripping the bottle of syrup, Mimi began to scream, "I didn't mean to! I DIDN'T MEAN TO!"

"To the pole" *He* said calmly.

Mimi took a few shorts steps and opened the basement door. She began to softly cry and whimper while peering down into the darkness. Looking back, *his* eyes piercing hers as she started to move her foot onto the first step. Every wooden stair creaked, as if to mock her with every move. The gaps between each step displayed a black abyss, *where the monster lives*, Mimi thought. Halfway down the stairs she saw the steel pole in the center of the basement. She moved slowly onto the concrete floor feeling every pebble and stone under her tender feet.

Mimi walked to the pole, carefully took off her shorts and underwear, and waited. Sometimes it took a while for *him* to come down. Distracted by the nearby toys, and with hardly enough light, Mimi reached for the Sit-n-Spin. Forgetting herself she sat down and folded her little legs around the turning handle. Feeling like someone was watching, she looked into a far corner of the basement. The corner near the other toys she likes to play with. Mimi called out, "hello?"

Mimi lost interest in the shadows in the corner and grabbed the handle of the Sit-n-Spin. Moving hand over hand, going faster and faster, Mimi lost herself in the swirling and spinning and then....STOP! *He* grabbed her by the hair and forced her back to the pole.

"HOLD IT!" *He* yelled as *he* pushed Mimi's hands to the freezing steel pole. She wrapped her hands around and waited. Hearing the clink of *his* belt, she tried to hold the pole. It was too late. She had already peed, and *He* was angrier, "such a fucking mess," *he* said. Every swing of the belt left a burning welt. Red hot and nearly bloody, Mimi fell to floor, crying, but *he* picked her up by her wrists and held her in place. *He* was determined to finish what he started. Now that she was crying, *he* would beat her until she stopped.

Chapter 15

The Closet

The softness from the winter coats and scarves floated over Mimi's skin, providing her a welcome refuge. *So much screaming*, she thought, *nobody ever shuts up*. Even Mimi, known to be the biggest screamer of them all, needed some *God-damned peace and quiet roun' here*, which were, ironically, so often the words spewing from *His* mouth.

Still rubbing her hands over the welts had she received just a few minutes before, Mimi felt as though the whole world disappeared when she went into the upstairs closet. It was long and smelled of cheap Avon perfume. When the house was particularly loud, Mimi could escape through the secret door in the very back. It was half the size of the regular door to get in, but perfect for a four-year-old. Beyond the coats and scarves and hard plastic suitcases, that little door beckoned Mimi.

"Closer, come closer," a voice whispered. Mimi opened the latch, stepped into the darkness, and found a seat on what she pretended to be a soft couch. The noise and busyness of the house could no longer be heard from beyond the closet.

"Do you like to play outside, Mimi?" The Voice asked.

"Yeah," Mimi whispered, not wanting anyone to hear her conversation and find her only secret place.

"Would you like to go outside and play right now?" The Voice paused for a moment and continued, "you can, you know."

Confused by such a statement, Mimi responded with a simple "no."

Playing outside would have meant leaving the secret place, having to walk past Him and the Stepmom and the boys and the others. She couldn't do that, not right now, it would have to wait. Besides, Mimi thought, *I don't want to leave you*, she pulled a nearby throw pillow close to her chest and rested her head on it.

The Voice was a soothing calm woman's voice and often echoed in Mimi's ears. Sometimes they are together, in a different space and time. A warm current rushed through Mimi's cold body; *She feels like a mommy.*

Mimi sat up and blurted out, "Can you be my Mommy?"

A short pause was followed by a gentle reply, "yes, I can be Mommy for you." Slouching back over the pillow, Mimi could feel Mommy's embrace. Warm pressure washed over her head, as if cradled in Mommy's sheltering hands. Finally feeling safe, Mimi drifted to sleep. Losing herself in the minutes and hours of the day, she woke to find herself once again, alone.

"Mommy?" Mimi calls. "Mommy?" She repeats her pleas, but the sound of her calls got smaller and smaller as she retreats to the elongated closet. Nobody missed her, nobody looked. It was past midnight, and the house was asleep. She slowly crept to the room she shared with the other kids.

Mimi climbed onto a bare mattress and tried to cover her cold feet with towel left on the bedroom floor. She wasn't quick enough to get a blanket tonight and she dared not wake anyone. As she stared out the massive window across from her bed, her thoughts quickly turned to Mommy and the trees she'd climb tomorrow.

Chapter 16

Journal Entry from Me – April 17, 2016

Mimi was held today, really held. To be four years old and not know it's like to be loved, and held, and cuddled, and warm; you don't know it's missing until it comes. Today, the love, the holding, the cuddling, and the warmth, it finally came. Mimi felt love in a way that we never thought was possible. To have someone be still and let us melt into her, V brought us healing today, and a little hope too. The idea of a future isn't a thing to a toddler, but it is to us. Today, the idea of being let out of our cerebral prison seemed possible. Mimi saw herself, out of the basement, out of the closet, and held by loving arms. She imagined for herself, for the first time, a different outcome; a new way of being and adored. It wasn't just for Mimi, I felt V's love too, and we long to be with her.

Chapter 17

Five-years-old

As a kid, I leaned into adventure. My neighborhood was a maze of catwalks. I learned how to ride a bike, climb trees, hop fences, roller skate, and went for long walks by myself. However, I was completely uncoordinated, accident prone, and easily lost. I loved being outside. There was nothing but trouble in the house. Going to school brought great relief during the winter months when playing outside became more challenging.

Off with the Pants

The summer I turned five-years-old I became aware of my "outsider" status. Parents of the children on my street sometimes allowed me to play in their homes but their kids were never permitted to play at mine. One day, neighborhood kids played near the front of my house. They gathered in groups with their bikes and roller skates. I had just come back from trying to join in with the roller-skating group with no success. They were older than me and despite my persistence, they refused citing I was slow and clumsy. Retreating in anger, I blazed a trail with my skates and went as fast as I could toward my house. I began to lose control and couldn't remember how to stop. As my upper body leaned forward, my legs buckled beneath me and down I went.

Tears began to well up and as quick as I could I went into the house to take off my skates. My knees were bloodied and bruised but my biggest worry was the pair of bright red polyester bell-bottoms that were now shredded at the knee and split in the crotch.

I threw my skates in the foyer closet, dried my tears, and went back outside. My hope of finding a friend to play with diminished as the kids who were still playing in front of our house began to laugh.

My embarrassment turned to anger. I stood next to a large Maple tree, reached down between my legs, found the hole that had formed and pulled as hard as I could. It took some time, but I managed to rip the pants completely off.

I drew more attention from the neighbors and the group of kids grew. They were pointing, laughing, calling their friends to come and see. My anger began to wane. *It was funny,* I thought and I began to laugh as well. I ran back into the house and put on my bright-blue polyester bell-bottoms, ran back outside and repeated my pants-shredding exhibit. It was the first time I felt out of control and crazy. It was also the first time I realized I could make friends by making them laugh.

I realize now their laughter was likely not the *with me* kind of laughter, they were laughing at me. In those moments, it didn't matter. My perception of their intent was enough to create in me the class jester. I could use what would naturally be embarrassing to my advantage. If I could laugh about my folly, nobody could touch me.

Chapter 18

The Wedding

He was familiar with the church building and the ones who called it their church home. *His* marriage to my mother meant *he* had a place in leadership when *he* wanted it. For a time *he* led the men's Bible study group and, on occasion, the adult Sunday School class.

Within a few months of my mother's passing, *He* married her best friend who also attended the small Baptist church. Legalistic Baptists who could claim generational ownership made up the majority of the congregation. The accepted doctrine of the church was that marriage was acceptable only under certain conditions. The death of a spouse meant no scrutiny when remarrying, however, when the marriage to my mother's best friend failed, *he* subsequently married yet another friend of *his* now ex-wife, the church made it uncomfortable for *him* to stay.

His intention was to remain in the church, but *his* image of 'charming widower' diminished when *his* pursuit of weak and desperate women became obvious. *He was* charming. *His* words were smooth and piercing, as *he* skillfully identified the needs of those around *him* and gained their trust by providing exactly the right thing. Making people believe *he* was a grieving widower who got saddled with two little girls was easy. *He* was a widower and *he* did have little girls. What people didn't see, or want to see, was what *he* was doing behind the scenes. *His* daughters were treated as animals or concubines, depending on *his* need. *His* wedding day to my second stepmother was the last time *he* attended that church, and the last time I danced on stage.

The final wedding day came and I felt beautiful in my fluffy white dress. It came to my knees and puffed out like a tutu. When I twirled it almost felt like I could take off into the air. I was proud of my white satin shoes; they were new, fit my feet, and buckled on the side. Ruffled white folded bobby socks were perfectly placed on each foot. It was special to be so dressed up. I knew it was a wedding but paid little attention to who was getting married.

My grandparents drove me and my sister to

the church. I loved being at the church. It was the only one I knew growing up. Grandma took me to church when nobody else was there and I found every tunnel, every closet, every secret door, and hidden rooms inside the walls. The secret doors and passageways made for endless adventures. I would pretend to be an explorer and seek out each room for treasure. *He* knew the church just as well as I did but it felt like it belonged to me and only me.

My favorite path was through the chapel. There was a door at the far end of the room that led to a dark hallway. I would run as fast as I could to reach the next door, swing it open, and immediately jump three giant steps down. Then there was a door to my right and stairs to my left. I usually went left. My little five-year-old legs would leap up each step until I reached my favorite place, the stage.

The stage was big, it stretched from one wall to the other. It was at the far end of the Fellowship Hall and was usually empty. On the day of the wedding, everyone was downstairs in the sanctuary when I, again, found myself on an adventure to the stage.

My new crisp white shoes made the perfect sound for some dancing, and I did not dance well, but

I did dance. I clipped and clacked my shoes and pointed my toes for dramatic effect. It didn't matter that there was no audience; I preferred it that way. I twirled my pretty white dress and raised my arms and hands like I had seen ballerinas do in a book my grandma used to read to me. I felt perfect joy. Until…I heard *His* voice.

He was calling for me. Frozen, my arms fell, legs tensed, and I felt the blood drain from my body. I felt warm liquid running down my legs, soaking my socks. *My pretty white socks*. My perfect new satin shoes, ruined. *I'm going to be in so much trouble*, I thought. Finding a bit of courage, I tried to be quick and run down the stairs. I crouched down hoping *he* wouldn't see me. It was no use.

Propped up in the corner were red and white canes clustered in a large barrel next to the stairs. They must have been part of some Christmas production. They looked like large candy canes without the hook on the end. *He* grabbed one of them and yelled at me to grab the railing. *He* lifted my pretty white dress and beat me. When *he* was done, *he* left me alone to clean myself up.

A short time later, my grandmother had found me in the bathroom. She took off my socks and underwear, put them in a plastic bag, and put my wet shoes back on my feet. I didn't feel pretty anymore. Grandma took me home with her for the night.

Chapter 19

New Stepmother

For about six months, both stepmothers and all their children lived in the house. The new stepmother had two kids who were close to my age. Over time, my stepbrother and I became close but my older stepsister and I, did not.

Things were fine for a bit after the previous stepmother and her kids moved out. The new stepmother spent a considerable amount of time telling her kids how great I was. "I would trade both my kids for one of Amy," she repeated to her friends. I felt special but it made my new siblings resentful.

The winter after they moved in, my stepbrother and I got into a minor fight. He and I walked outside, he pushed me into picker-bushes, and I promptly called him a "bitch." He ran inside screaming for his mom.

That word was flung back and forth between *Him* and Stepmom at least four times a day. Fearing *Him* more, I followed my stepbrother into the house to plead my case. Stepmom was standing at the door in a fuzzy green robe that was open enough to see her silk nighty.

"Did you call my son a bitch?" her tiny face wrinkled up under her frizzy red hair.

In usual fashion, I tried to explain what her son had done. She said nothing more but instead smacked me, hard, across my face.

In between moments of hatred for all children, but particularly directed at me and my older half-sister, my new stepmom was nice. I was a very compliant child and attempted to anticipate every need. I spent the next few years serving coffee, making meals, cleaning the house, rubbing *His* feet, and lighting cigarettes, all at the request of my parents and their friends. It became a running joke for their friends to refer to me as Cinderella. As long as I did what I was told, life was okay. At times when Stepmom would tire of me, if I didn't match the socks right, wipe under the toaster, or I played too loudly, she slapped me in the face. - I remained loyal.

Chapter 20

Dinner

Our one meal came in the evening, when hungry bellies and chattering children surrounded the large dining room table. We all took our places along the sides of the table. The large chairs with their stilt backs and staunch, ornate wooden arms, made it difficult to sit in any position but the 'proper' one; butt in chair, elbows off the table and feet on floor (if you were tall enough to touch the floor). I swung my feet with ease until an ankle met with a wooden crossbar at the bottom of the chair. Forgetting ourselves and our manners, an elbow may creep onto the table, or God-forbid someone chewed with their mouth open. Those moments brought swift action, with a smack across the face, or a quick swat to the back of the head. How quickly we all remembered our manners then.

Dinner time was an orchestrated game put on by *Him* and whichever stepmother *he* was married to at the time. We were expected to set the table and do it properly: plate center, glass to the upper left, butter knife and spoon to the left on the napkin, fork to the right of the plate. Everything had to be just so. I don't know if this is the proper 'English' way, though *He* liked to pretend we were some kind of elite group that could entertain the Queen of England should she happen to be in the neighborhood.

The rules of game the changed depending on *His* mood. Could we sit before or after *he* did? Could we speak at the dinner table? *His* inquisitions about what happened at school and who told what to what teacher were endless, yet no one dare utter anything other than a simple "yes" or "no." Some nights *he* displayed a jolly demeanor and joked with a few of us forgetting all that happened from day to day. Only a few understood it was a precursor for what was coming later that evening.

All the fancy place-settings in the world could not dress up our nightly serving of thick-sliced fried bologna on white bread or, if it were a real occasion, baked hotdogs packed with mashed potatoes with cheese on top. To this day I cannot eat bologna. The smell of it makes my throat tighten.

It was hard not to gobble up all the food once

it hit the table but there were consequences for everything. Never knowing what was going to be praised or punished that day kept us on our toes. Could we serve ourselves tonight or wait for a designated servant? The server was usually chosen by age and whoever had been in the most trouble that day. I was rarely called on to serve. I was clumsy and absent-minded. It was difficult to not spill the lemonade, it was always lemonade, while going from glass to glass. One of the older kids usually poured. If they spilled, smack! If they said something under their breath, smack! If their hair got on the table, a quick yank to remind them of their manners was swift. There wasn't any time between offense and punishment. We rarely saw it coming. Most nights there was dinner on the table. Even if it was processed pig parts and white bread, it was food. Day time was different.

Most days we woke up and went right outside even if it wasn't ideal weather conditions. When it was too cold, the only obstacle was the lack of thick coats, shoes, gloves, hats, basically everything you need to play outside when it's freezing. Michigan is cold from October through March, but I wasn't about to stay inside if I could help it. I found things to put on, even when they weren't mine. I rummaged through the foyer closet and found giant coats and sloppy boots, anything to get out of the house. No gloves or mittens shielded my hands from the bitter snow but I built snow forts and snowmen anyhow. I often dug out clumps of ice from the inside of my boots.

When lunchtime came around there may be some lemonade sent outside by Stepmom. All of us would take turns drinking from the top of the pitcher. When we had our fill we would leave it on the porch and set out to keep playing. There may be a package of saltines sent with the lemonade but this was not typical. On days when there were crackers we felt alive and left our simple lunch with renewed energy.

Some days, with little or nothing to eat, we were sapped of life and stayed inside to play in the basement or in our bedrooms. The basement was full of sticky, dank, plastic toys. My bedroom didn't have much of anything except a large box I could climb up to see out the window and into the backyard. My room had a special door tucked into the bottom of the wall. The door was small where only the littlest ones could fit, but some days the only way out of that house was to get into the walls. The other hidden door on the second floor was through the hall closet and it had what we needed.

The hall closet held odds and ends, remnants

of days long past for Stepmom. Fur coats, scarves, blankets, and a leather biker jacket hung from racks along the sides of the closet walls. Large round boxes teetered from the top shelves, almost screaming for me to climb a stack of suitcases, open the boxes and set free whatever poor animal had been frozen in time.

Stealing away to the hall closet took some finesse. We had to wait until everyone was asleep or occupied with other things. During the day it was difficult to sneak around, *Him* and Stepmom purposefully set out to play "capture the rat." *We* were the rats. But, sometimes, when the house was quiet, maybe *he* had taken a few of the kids to the store, gone for a walk or maybe she had drunk too much vodka with her daily helping of pills and fallen asleep, I could open the hall closet door, gently flip the light switch on, and settle in under the coats.

The suitcases were strictly forbidden by Stepmom and one day I found out why. She had belonged to a multi-level marketing company that sold erotic toys and candy.

One afternoon, when the weather was more than egregious, it was below zero and we were relegated to playing indoors. I stole away to my favorite spot under the furs and began to open a suitcase. The slide-latch on the hardtop, olive green, case made a snapping noise that I was sure would draw some attention. I paused for a moment and then lifted the heavy lid. Lying on the very top were square wrappers that did not appeal to me but when I lifted them up, I caught a glimpse of shiny penises, big ones, some black and some pink. I picked up a black one and put it to my mouth and then took a bite. The aroma of chocolate and a thick swirl of milky goodness filled my mouth. I didn't know they could taste like that. The hunger pangs began to subside as I took bite after delicious bite. The richness of the chocolate forced me to slow down but I had to hurry. I knew this was forbidden.

The closet door swung open. Stepmom stood there. Her face as red as her hair. I knew I had eaten when I wasn't supposed to, but I didn't know I had "stolen money" by eating her precious product. My head stung as she wrapped my hair around her boney fingers and yanked me from the closet. I don't remember what happened after that.

Chapter 21

Six with V

"How are you today?" V asked.

V stood in the doorway of her office. She was waiting for the coffee to fill her cup and leaned over to check its progress.

"I'm okay."

I walked in her office and saw that she had already set out our family diagram on the table in the center of the rom. I sat on the loveseat. V left for a moment to retrieve her drink. She entered the room, sat down next to me and asked, "are you sure?"

"I just feel off. I don't know. Like, my head is fuzzy, and I can't get my hair to do anything. It feels gross. No matter how many times I wash it, it won't come clean."

V placed her cup on the table and touched my hair. It hung down past my shoulders. "It feels okay and looks okay too." She sat back and looked at it again.

"Have any of you," pointing at the family diagram, "had trouble with your hair when you were little?"

I knew what she was doing. We had spent months going over some of the hard stuff in my past and the hard stuff from the other kids too. Every emotion and body pain V attributed to something deeply rooted in the past. She was probably right but most days I really didn't know what the others knew or what they had been through. I knew some things but they told her their stories on their own visits. How was I to know?

"I don't know a ton about it, but Six had issues with her hair." I slunk into the cushion and pretended like I didn't care that we were talking about *them*, again.

"Tell me more. And tell me why her name is Six again?"

"None of us were really known by our names. *He* called *his* Brood. *He* called the girls, Son. Some of us were just known by our ages, like Six and Eight. *He* called me Anus for a while, I'm not sure why. Maybe *he* just thought it was funny. Stepmom called me Grace because I tripped over nothing at all. We were never sure what our name would be on any given day."

"Hmmmm," a look of concern came to V. "Tell me about Six and her hair."

Chapter 22

Hair Cut

Bath time happened every Sunday before bed. The oldest child filled the bathtub with warm water and one by one, all the kids in the house would take a bath in the same water. A new layer of filth was left behind by each. By the time Six got in the tub, the water was cold and brown.

Six was the shyest of all the kids. Hunger kept her from moving too fast or speaking out of turn. Lack of nourishment kept her mind slow. Six leaned against the wall, stepped out of the tub and grabbed the shared towel laying on the floor. It was wet from the others who had bathed before her.

Despite her best attempt at drying off, Six's hair continued to drip on the floor. She methodically put on the same dirty white tank top and oversized underwear she had been wearing and this was the third day she couldn't find clean clothes. Sunday routines included going downstairs where Stepmom was waiting in her recliner. Each child went to Stepmom to get their hair brushed. A dreaded task for all.

"Hurry up and get your ass down here," Stepmom's voice echoed throughout the house.

Six moved as fast as she could without losing balance on the stairs. Stepmom sat, legs wide open, on her favorite brown corduroy recliner. She held a brush in one hand and a lit cigarette in the other. Six, shivering, took her place on the floor in between Stepmom's legs.

"Hold still." Stepmom gripped the large wooden handle and pushed the wire brush into Six's scalp.

"Ouch." Six put her hand to her head as Stepmom pulled the brush down.

"Shut up." She said. Striking Six on the top of the head with the brush.

Tears welled. Six pulled her knees to her chest

and began to cry.

"Just go to bed. You're not worth it."
Stepmom sat back in her chair and puffed her
cigarette. She moved her foot to Six's back and gave
her a shove. "GO!"

Six climbed into the bottom bunk and covered
her cold body with a small blanket. She wiped her
face and fell asleep.

A couple hours later, Stepmom came to Six's
room, flipped on the overhead light and said, "wakey,
wakey." She grabbed Six by the arm and pulled her
from bed. "Basement!" She glared at Six but Six kept
her eyes to the ground. With her hand on the back of
Six's neck, Stepmom directed her down the two
flights of stairs to the basement. Confident she was
destined for the pole, Six walked unassisted toward
the pole, but Stepmom pushed her past it and into the
laundry area.

Six tried to keep her teeth from chattering.
The bitter cold of the basement was nearly unbearable
as Six was still only wearing a thin tank and loose
underwear.

"Sit," Stepmom said.

Six sat on the stool, pressed her knees together, and wrapped her arms around her chest.

"Quit fidgeting. I swear." Stepmom walked behind Six and grabbed a large chunk of hair.

"You're disgusting. You bathe and you're still dirty. Did you even brush your teeth?" Stepmom pulled out a large pair of fabric scissors and began to cut close to Six's scalp.

Pressing her hands to her face, Six wept.

"I'd pull out your teeth if I could." Stepmom was manic. She chopped of chunks of Six's hair until only about an inch was left. "Disgusting." She put the scissors in the blue washtub and gave Six a shove, motioning for her to get off the stool. "You can sleep down here for the rest of the night."

Stepmom went upstairs and Six made her way to the couch on the opposite end of the basement. Six laid down and stared out a small window high on the adjacent concrete wall. Still crying, she fell asleep gripping her now short hair.

The next day, Six woke to the sound of the basement door opening. Slow, soft steps alerted Six to get out of view. *I don't want anyone to see me*, she thought. It was Mimi. Six quickly moved to the corner under the window. The sun streaming in from the window made the corner underneath it, dark. Six watched as Mimi took off her pants and underwear at the pole. *She's in bad trouble*. Six then watched as Mimi moved over to the Sit-n-Spin and began to play. *She's going to be in real bad trouble.* "Mimi, get up," Six whispered. Mimi peered into the corner but Six didn't move. *He's coming*. Six slid down the wall and crouched and watched as *He* spanked Mimi at the pole.

Chapter 23

He's Here for Six

"Six? Oh, Six? Come out, come out wherever you are." *He* was in the basement and Six had nowhere else to hide. There are only a few really dark places in the basement, and *he* knew where to find her. Six was obedient. She followed every command and never questioned why she didn't have a name.

Six had been hiding in the shadows behind the water heater. *He* spotted her and she began to walk toward *him*.

"I brought you some lemonade. You been down here for a bit, I imagine you're thirsty."

Six grabbed the plastic cup and gulped, the lemonade dripped down her chin.

"Oops, guess you were, huh?" *He* took the cup

from her and placed it on the dryer.

"Come'n?" *He* put his arm around her shoulders and led her to the hole.

Six laid stiff under the stairs. *Him* and her in the hole, a hidden place under the basement stairs. It was dingy, had blankets stacked on the bottom and an old blanket tacked to the top, it was used to shut out the rest of the world. Light from the spaces in-between the stair steps came through in a crisscross pattern.

"Six, can you hear me?" The Voice crossed time and space to reach her.

"Six?"

"Six? Come on sweetheart, come back. Can you hear me?"

Warmth rushed through Six's body. The basement was cold and Six's even more cold because of her nakedness. Six looked up and saw a florescent light streaming through a burlap sack draped and then tucked around her head. Concentrating on the pattern;

crisscross, crisscross, crisscross, crisscross…. Six was no longer able to hear the distant beckoning of The Voice. Six was with *Him* now.

Six managed to wiggle the top half of her body out of the hole, but the rest of her was still in there, with *Him*. She wanted to scream. Go back to her shadows. Her legs spread wide to accommodate *his* thighs, and arms stretched out by her sides. She couldn't move, every muscle tight, stuck. *He* began to hum a nursery rhyme. Six heaved her chest to scream, but no noise came out.

Six heard the clanking and scraping of metal. The basement smelled of dirt, *his* sweat, and rubbing alcohol. Not enough to distract her from the pain. Piercing, ice cold, pain. On the left. Now the right. Between her legs and then, thick and warm fluid, flowing down her inner thigh. *He* had cut her. Gasping and then releasing her breath, Six broke out into a cold sweat, making the cold of the basement air unbearable against her body. She felt the pebbles and dirt scrap against her back as *he* grabbed her calves and pulled her further into the hole. She found two small rocks on the floor and rolled them between her fingers.

"Six? Can you hear me?" The Voice called a

bit more urgent now. Six was quickly transported into the tender embrace of a mother.

Don't see me. Don't see me. Don't see me. Six closed her eyes and wished herself away.

Me with V

"Amy?" V's voice broke through the sound of distant humming. V's hands were warm and wrapped around me like I was a child.

"I'm okay." I wasn't okay. I felt empty, blank, and confused. I sat up, ran my fingers through my hair and took a piece of chocolate off the table in front of us.

"I think we should wrap things up," V said.

"Wow, that was fast. I guess we can talk about my hair next time."

I stood up and felt as if my head would touch the ceiling. I felt ten feet tall. My body didn't work the way it should. My legs were too long, and V had shrunk. Still feeling the remnants of a child, I moved awkwardly toward the door. It would be another week before we met with V. We longed to be with her.

Chapter 24

Jacob and the Snakes

By the time second grade rolled around, Jacob and I had become really good friends but also fierce competitors. Jacob climbed trees, fences, and even scaled brick homes in his bare feet. I was tall, uncoordinated, and clumsy but I was also very strong. I could always beat him in a fight as long as no running was involved.

Jacob and I spent many days playing outside, exploring the neighborhood, and often walked to school together. At seven years old, both Jacob and I tagged along on a job that his mother had as the caretaker of a cemetery. At the front of a 13-acre graveyard sat a large 5-bedroom farmhouse. Grey paint was peeling off the siding. There was a large access door to the basement off the back of the house.

In the center of the yard was a willow tree, the kind that looked like it had been there for two-hundred years. Its trunk was so large, it made a perfect hiding place for playing Ghost in Graveyard, a game Jacob's cousins had made up. Stepmom often brought her friends and some family over to the house to drink and play cards. The children would go outside and play. Ghost in the Graveyard was just like Hide and Go Seek with a spooky name to match the location.

Our days at the graveyard often began in the early afternoon and stretched on through the night depending on how many people showed up to play cards. One particular afternoon, Jacob and I had come with Stepmom. *He* had come this time as well but no one else had arrived yet. Jacob and I went exploring. We weren't big fans of hanging around the headstones and it took great effort not to step on the ones that were flat and had been sucked into the earth.

The graveyard had been established in the 1800s and it was creepy. The headstones varied in size, many unreadable but the creepiest part were the dozens of small mausoleums spread throughout the property. At night, the graveyard seemed to come alive. Jacob and I kept close to the old willow tree at night and rarely ventured beyond the first row of headstones.

Before everyone arrived that day, Jacob and I walked down to the ravine near the road. It had been lightly raining on and off for several days and the water began to gather at the bottom. We did our best not to slip on our way down. We held onto each other's shirts and went sideways for more stability. Once we reached the bottom, Jacob gleefully jumped into the water. It came up to his knees. Quickly realizing the mud under the water had trapped his shoes, he called for me to help pull him out. After I stopped laughing, I carefully entered the water and grabbed his hand. I tugged on his arm a few times and finally Jacob was able to free his feet from the mud. Unfortunately, his shoes remained submerged in the mud.

Jacob didn't care that he would get in trouble for losing his shoes. His attention was drawn elsewhere.

"Did you see it?" He asked.

"See what?" I asked and looked down at the area of the water he was pointing.

"A snake!"

"I'm getting outta here," I said and then began to back my way up the hill to the yard.

"I bet you, you can't even catch one. You're such a pussy."

I turned sharply and stared at him.

"Oh, yeah. Watch me," I said.

Again sideways, I shimmied down to the bottom of the ravine. I did not like snakes, but I wasn't about to have him show me up either. I rolled up my sleeves and stuck both of my hands in the murky water. I could feel them sliding around my ankles and through my fingers. I took a deep breath and closed my fists.

"I got two! I got two!" I screamed.

I immediately began running back to the house to show *Him*. I was proud of my capture, and I wanted to show *him* I could do boy stuff too. Jacob followed behind me. I ran across the yard holding both snakes with my arms outstretched as far as they would go. When I reached the back door to the house,

I waited for Jacob to open the door. I stepped in and saw *Him* and Stepmom sitting at the kitchen table.

"Guess what? Guess what?" I asked. I was excited to show off my conquest.

"What?" *He* asked.

"Look! I caught snakes! I did it and Jacob said I couldn't do it but I did."

"Then where are they?" *He* asked.

I looked at my outstretched arms and realized I must have let go of the snakes somewhere between the back door and the kitchen. Just then, Stepmom screamed, "what the hell?"

Two green garter snakes slithered across the kitchen floor, under the table, and then into a hole under the cabinets along the wall. Stepmom's fear turned into fury.

"I'm not in the mood for this shit," Stepmom stated.

"Go outside and pick a switch and not the short ones," *He* said.

He was talking to both me and Jacob. I had gotten Jacob into trouble. I didn't mean to. Jacob and I went back outside and went to the old willow tree. *He* was close behind.

"Not that one," *He* barked.

I put down a stick I had just picked up and chose the one *He* pointed to. The daylight was almost gone, and it began to lightly rain. Under the old willow tree Jacob and I were punished, Jacob for losing his shoes and me for being absent-minded and impulsive. We were directed to go in the house and sit quietly for the rest of the night. It wasn't long before Jacob's cousins began to show up. There would be no playing in the graveyard that night.

Jacob and I sat on the hard wood floor against the wall in the living room. We could see and hear the adults in the kitchen as they played cards. Jacob took my hand and didn't let go all night. We whispered jokes to each other, and Jacob forced out burps to make me laugh. They never did catch those snakes.

Me with V

"It sounds like Jacob was a really good friend," V said.

"Yeah, he was. I miss him. I don't know what happened to him after everyone left."

"When did everyone leave?"

"When I was around ten years old, I think. It was like, poof, everyone vanished."

V glanced at the clock. She doesn't ever think I notice but I do. I tend to leave her office later than when I'm supposed to. She never complains. I wish I knew where the time went. I spend too much time in empty spaces and waste all the minutes I have with her.

"I should go," I said.

"Okay. Maybe we can talk more about this little one next time?" V picked up a picture of Eight.

"Yeah, I guess but I don't know too much about her. There were only a couple of pictures of her."

I gathered my things and headed home. Still confused about the conversations V seems to be having without me. It's my time. It doesn't seem right. It all gets sucked away. *Oh well, it's fine,* I told myself. *We'll see her next week.*

Chapter 25

Eight-years-old

Summer had passed and school began. I was in the third grade and grateful for the structure of the day. Lined with mature maple, pine, and birch trees the walk to school became an adventure. Fall had drifted in; the air was crisp. I picked up pinecones, yellow and red leaves, and half-eaten acorns the squirrels left behind.

Some days I carried a few books, early readers that I couldn't read and notebooks with my name, "Amy," spelled backwards. Occasionally, if Stepmom remembered to pack it the night before, I took a lunchbox. It was green with a superhero cartoon on the front. The details of the graphic mostly hidden by layers of dirt.

One day in October, Stepmom had set out the lunchboxes on the half-wall and I, happy to ease my growling belly, took mine and began walking to school.

With my arms full, I reached down to pick up pinecones. I set the lunchbox on the sidewalk, opened the latch, hoping the pinecones would fit. The familiar smell of mold crept out. I moved the juice and crackers over and put the new treasures in my box. Most kids got to school in fifteen minutes, but my treasure hunting doubled my time.

Two massive pine trees hung over the sidewalk as a I rounded the last corner. My brick ranch style elementary school appeared. Activity swirled. Busy parents were dropping off their kids. Children rushed to the playground for one quick swing before the bell, while teachers scolded them for their blatant disregard for time efficiency.

Conscious of my treasures and books, I slowly pushed open the door. Karen, a sixth grader, towered over me and held the door. She was the tallest girl in school and had straight bright red hair that flowed to her hips. Karen's face and arms were covered with freckles. Always happy to see me, her gums protruded when she smiled.

Karen befriended me on the first day of

school. I had gotten lost in the halls after coming out of the bathroom. She showed me how to get to the library where my teacher had taken the class for story hour. I found myself in the library often that year, it was a place of solace. The tightly lined bookshelves provided cover from the peering eyes of my teacher. Expansive and soft, the red carpet bounced as it glided over different levels. A square reading pond was centered at the bottom level.

Keeping the door from closing shut, Karen's wide smile let me know I was free to let go and keep walking.

"Thanks," I said in a sheepish tone.

"No prob," she quipped, as if to pat me on the head with her words.

The echo of children's voices, laughs, and whispers all merged into one. I walked down one hall and then another. My classroom was on the right and the coat racks were outside the room. A long shelf spanned from one classroom door to another, the area where students dutifully placed their lunchboxes. The business of the morning was interrupted by the long sound of the school bell. Students hurried into their classrooms. I quickly took note of where my treasures were on the shelf, and everyone else's too. I walked to my seat.

I entered a large classroom. My seat was next to a window that looked out onto the playground. I put my books on the desk and sat down. Tugging at my blue polka dotted dress, I tried to cover the rips in my dirty off-white tights. It was picture day.

Lunch time was getting closer. My head was fuzzy. The teacher had scolded me all morning for paying more attention to the birds outside than the lessons. Nothing made sense. Her words bounced around my head until tears streamed down my face.

"You're a daydreamer, little girl. Wake UP!" Her sharp tone matched her stiff permed hair.

Don't look at her, a voice inside crept in, *don't look*.

"Can I go to the bathroom?" I managed to squeak out.

Her sharp voice interrupted, "May I?"

I stuttered, "Sorry. May, may, may, may I go please?"

She reached around and grabbed a hall pass from her desk. I could feel twenty-eight pair of eyes on me as I walked out into the hallway. A quick turn to the left, I reached up and grabbed the first lunchbox off the shelf. Almost running, I went into the bathroom, opened a stall, sat on the floor, and opened the lunchbox. Nervous and hungry, I pulled out a peanut butter and jelly sandwich and took massive bites. I opened the juice box and took a big gulp to get the last of the sandwich down my throat. The stall door swung open hard. It hit the wall and bounced back. My legs wouldn't move. I saw the bottom of a dress as my teacher pulled me up by my arm.

"What are you doing?" My teacher shouted. She pulled me down the hall to the principal's office moving so fast I lost one of my favorite patent leather shoes. It would later be returned but not before all hell broke loose.

What came next was a haze of phone calls. I could hear my teacher and the principal speaking behind closed doors, and then *He* came. I had been in trouble before for not doing my homework or paying attention and from time-to-time forgetting what I had already learned. Everyone seemed perplexed by my ineptitude.

I sat in a chair against the wall, facing the secretary while *He* talked to the principal in a separate office. Desperate to disappear, I tugged and pulled at my dress. *I can't believe they called Him*, I thought. A few minutes passed, the door opened, and the principal called my name. My chest sank. Still with only one shoe, I walked awkwardly into the office. The principal said something to *Him* and then left. The door shut. *He* took off his belt.

"You be quiet, or we'll continue this at home." He pushed me toward the desk and lifted my dress. Puffs of air were all I let out with each blow. My head was fuzzy. Tears and snot ran down my cheeks and into my mouth. I don't remember *him* leaving or me returning to class but I know I remained in school for the rest of the day.

Somewhere between the office and the end of the day, I had gotten my shoe back, and walked home. I was sent to my room for the rest of the evening. Holding onto my lunchbox, I was grateful my treasures remained. Juice and crackers were my dinner that night.

Chapter 26

Eight's Basement

It was an unusually warm day for early Spring. Eight's legs stuck to the leather car seat as they drove through winding dirt roads and then into a neighborhood. Eight sat behind *Him.* Her usual position was next to *Him* in the front seat. *He's mad at me again*, she thought. Mid-Winter break from school had pushed *him* to the edge. There were several children to contend with and Eight was headstrong, sarcastic, and often got popped in the mouth for her impulsive quips. *His* attempts to break her and make her compliant and *his*, like *he* boasted with *his* other children, had not worked with Eight. She was what Grandma called, spirited.

Eight leaned her head against the window and looked out at the passing fields of rural Michigan. *He* began talking to someone, maybe Eight but nothing *he* said made sense. It felt like *he* was talking to someone else. *His* tone reflected a deep conversation and *his* hands gestured as if explaining something profound but no one else was in the car.

The dirt road ended and *He* and Eight slowly drove through a middle-class neighborhood. *He* pulled into a driveway and Eight sat up to get a better look. They had pulled into the driveway of a two-story white colonial. Manicured bushes on each side of an ornate archway shrouded the front door. The home's many angles and climbing ivy set it apart from its mid-century brick neighbors.

Placing the car in park, *He* left the keys in the ignition and stepped out. Eight opened her door, peeled her bare thighs from the leather seat and together they walked toward the house. A tall man stood under a metal carport. He had a round belly that stuck out of his red plaid cotton t-shirt. The man talked to *Him* for a few minutes and then *he* placed *his* hand on Eight's back and told the man, "Here, you can have this one too."

Eight tilted her head and looked at the front door. *He* got in the car and left as the man from the driveway led Eight to the door. They walked under the archway and into the shadow of the bushes. Just inside to the right stood a woman washing dishes. Intent on completing the task the woman never acknowledged Eight's presence.

Straight ahead were basement stairs. Eight walked down one step, then two, then three. She hesitated and looked back at the man. His belly in her face, there was no going back up. A veil of black shadow concealed the remaining steps. Eight walked into an abyss.

Just beyond the black, sudden pressure around her waist and a bristly hand over her mouth. Someone had caught her off guard and swept her off the stairs. Her legs violently kicked at the air. She tried to scream and then everything disappeared.

Unaware if it was the same day or how much time had passed, Eight opened her eyes, sucked in her chest and frantically put her hand up to hold the ceiling. She felt as though the floor from the room above was crushing her. The small space she was in was collapsing. Eight's throat tightened. She managed to let out a low scream. Several moments passed before realizing the room was not getting smaller. She had been shoved into a crawl space of a Michigan basement. Cascading cement, large boulders, and dirt cylinders prevented her from laying straight. Eight's body contorted around the frame of the century old foundation. She gasped for air as someone grabbed her ankles and yanked. Her back scrapped along the dirt as she slid out through the opening. Once again, Eight was unconscious.

Eight opened her eyes. Someone had moved her again. *Dead. I'm dead.* No noise, no light, no smell, no air, death was the only explanation. Eight became aware of her quick, shallow breathing and a fullness in her lower belly. The sensation of floating was followed by the sound of plastic dragging along the ground. She floated with the sounds of the dragging. *Not dead. Not dead. They're gonna kill me.*

Episodes of wake and sleep continued for the next five days. Awake, ropes on Eight's ankles and wrists. A cold hard table underneath her. Nothing to cover her shame and nakedness. At the foot of the table, there they were. Shadows. Three of them. Cloaked in black. There to break her. *He* had enlisted *his* friends to do the job *he* failed to do. *He* failed to make her obedient and to make her loyal.

Discussing their plans, the shadows conducted their meeting as if in a boardroom. They collaborated on the torture; what kind, how long, and who would do what. They appeared as shadows but were faceless and cold humans cloaked in robes symbolizing their religious membership. To them Eight was an object or an animal, a project.

Eight's feet began to throb from the stick they used to keep her awake. The shadows wanted compliance. *Nope, not me*, Eight thought, *they got 'em all but not me*. She was exhausted from no food and the "medicine" they added to her water. Eight couldn't physically fight, though she wanted to. They wanted her to break but she held on. *He* wanted loyalty but Eight would not bend. Lying flat on the stone table, Eight's breathing changed. Her chest heaved up then down. Her nostrils flared with each exhale. *He told them to break me. No! I hate them! I hate them! I hate Him!*

Eight squinted from intermittent flashes of the swinging overhead lights. A blank look came over her face, her hands drooped off the sides of the table, and her breathing slowed. Unable to remain in herself Eight turned her head to the left and focused on the wall decoration. An eight-foot tapestry with an ornate gold border and in the center, two little boys hanging upside down. They were naked and lifeless until a breeze or some force made their bodies sway forward and back, forward and back. *It's just a painting. It's just a painting*. Eight curled her fingers and scrapped them along the stone beneath her. *It's just a painting.*

The basement holds terrors of which can hardly be describe. Five days of torture, burns, cutting, chanting, planning, and hanging. Five days. A simple work week for the shadows. They went back to their normal lives. Five days. He appeared again, the man from the beginning. Eight floated behind and watched him carry her limp body up the stairs. Feeling accomplished somehow; *we won. We beat the game*, Anna proclaimed. Eight remained in the basement, Anna emerged victorious. Anna: compliant, obedient, loyal.

Me With V

"That sounds really hard," V put her hand on mine.

"I guess," I said.

"Oh, you're freezing."

V pulled a blanket from the back of the loveseat and wrapped me up like a mother wrapping a sick child.

I felt stunned and like I had just emerged from under water. Tears had soaked V's shirt. I didn't realize I had been crying that hard or for how long V had been holding me. Not me, I guess, but Eight. She rarely came to see V and when she did, I slipped away.

"Sorry, sorry, there's no more," I managed to utter.

Flashes of rope sprung up in my mind. Two little boys swinging from the ceiling and moments of terror in a dark cavern played on repeat. My body was abnormally cold. I pulled the white crocheted blanket in closer. I shook my head back and forth as tears began to fall again. V pulled me in close to her.

"I'm so sorry that happened to you," V said. Her tone was soft and slow. "I'm so sorry. You're here now. You survived. You made it."

Not me. It wasn't me, I thought. *She's not me. I'm not her. It didn't happen. Just a dream.*

"It did happen," Anna said loudly. Raising her head from V's chest, "it did happen."

"I know it did, sweety. I know it did." V sat back for a moment. "Who do I have here?"

Confused by her lack of recognition, Anna always thought herself to be V's favorite, "It's me. It's Anna," she said. Anna settled her head on V's shoulder.

"Oooh," V's voice became brighter. "It's so nice to see you, Anna. Thank you for telling me. Were you helping Eight tell her story?"

Anna sat up, smiled and nodded yes. "Eight's scared."

"Where is Eight?" V asked. "Can she come and talk to me?"

"No, she's in the basement," Anna said. "Eight stayed in the basement. She's there." Anna cocked her head to the side knowing that she was the result of Eight's time in the basement. The shadows wanted Anna. *He* wanted Anna. Eight stayed and Anna emerged to take her place.

"Well, tell her she can talk to me any time she

wants," V said.

"Okay."

Anna held the vision of Eight and the basement in her mind. Anna pictured herself standing beside Eight. Anna bent over and whispered in Eight's ear, "we'll be back later for you."

Anna sat up a bit and then leaned into V once more.

Eight is still in the basement. She waits for rescue. She can hear V's voice from time to time. Eight is afraid to come out of the dark and into V's arms. We are hoping one day Eight will emerge and stay with us.

Chapter 27

Summer

The summer after third grade I was sent to live with my grandparents for a month. My grandmother made sure my days were valuable and productive. She taught me how to cook, garden, sing, play piano, and oil paint. Her house was full of adventure. I walked barefoot on cool stones in her rock garden. Hostas, ferns, and tropical looking orange and red flowers filled the gaps between the large stones. Frogs and toads moved quickly from rock to rock. I was careful to not step on any bugs in the thick brush. They were my friends. Not the bees. Grandpa always said, "bees are assholes."

Raspberries bushes grew with little resistance along the back fence. They seemed bigger every year spreading their thin fingers across the back and sides of a wooden shed. Sweet bursts of raspberries were enough to get me to squeeze between the thorn covered branches and reach for the biggest ones I could find. It was a delicate dance sliding back out

into the open yard without squishing the berries
between my fingers or scratching my bare skin
against the razor-sharp thorns.

Grandma's garden was her pride and joy that
summer. My grandmother stood in the middle of the
garden and the corn towered over her. She was happy
to show off her perfectly ripened tomatoes when
company came. Grandma was very popular at church.
Her friends and their husbands popped by nearly
every day. Grandpa didn't seem to mind the
company. He had a fancy woodshop in the garage and
loved to show the men around while the women
drank iced tea and ate coffee cake on the back deck.

Grandpa was a tall, sturdy man, and he loved
me. I inherited his hair. It was strawberry blond,
curly, and thick. My hair was so heavy and there was
so much of it, by the time I was five, the curls had
relaxed into waves and the blond became a golden
brown. Grandma and Grandpa couldn't seem to get
enough of me, and I of them.

My time with my grandparents that summer
came to an abrupt end when they dropped me off at a
tiny little house in an urban subdivision. Without
warning *Him* and Stepmom had packed all of our
things and moved. The next two months, we stayed in

a two-bedroom rental home while our new house was being built.

The rental house was located in a rundown city just outside the Detroit city limits. Our street was lined with small bungalows that had once been occupied by auto workers. The auto industry had greatly diminished in Detroit and the occupants were now low-income renters, most of them on welfare or disability. The houses, like the adults who lived in them, appeared broken, dirty, sad, and worn out. Our street was the only one that had not been paved. The ditches held random garbage, food wrappers, cigarette butts, and if us kids were lucky, returnable pop bottles.

Random chain link fences created a maze of gates and crooked lines up and down the street. Our house, one of the few without a fence, had chalky blue asbestos siding, and no porch or back yard. All of us kids shared one bedroom and *Him* and Stepmom slept in the other bedroom off the kitchen.

Upon entry into our tiny summer cottage, you were immediately dumped into the living room, only big enough for a small couch. My summer days and sometimes nights, were spent outside. If I wasn't asleep, I was walking up and down the dirt road looking for stray cats to befriend. In the morning I headed to the corner store for Stepmom's daily pack of cigarettes. A short, hand-written note was all that was required for a nine-year-old to buy cigarettes. I rarely wore shoes. I had to go slow long the road, but the coolness of the dirt felt good in the summer heat. It felt good to be outside. It felt good to have freedom. The best part was that there were children my age in the neighborhood and they were weird too. We spent many of our days playing tag and riding on a tiny dirt bike with no brakes. My dirt bike riding days came to an end when the second time I had gotten on the bike, I lost control, spun out and got my head stuck under a chain link fence.

The Fourth of July rolled around. The neighborhood was all abuzz with the coming holiday. All the families on our street gathered on their porches. Myself, Stepmom, and two of my siblings sat on the neighbor's stoop. Someone had purchased a ton of fireworks and the center of our street became the biggest firework show in the city that night. The smoke was thick. The smell of sulfur filled my nose, I didn't care. It meant fun and friends. BOOM! Another explosion of blue and red lights shredded high in the air. The next firework lit was smaller and swirled around in a circle. Through the smoke, I saw a small light quickly heading my way and then bam, I felt a thunk on my forehead. Stepmom started to scream, "her hair's on fire!" Sure enough, the latest light display had played out its greatest trick on my head. I didn't see fire but heard my hair sizzling. I began swatting my head.

"Fucking retard!" Stepmom yelled. Her beer washed over my head and face. Her kids started to laugh, and then I joined in. The neighbors stood stoic as the firework show was briefly paused.

"You okay?" one of the neighbors asked.

"Yeah."

Unconcerned with my singed hair I ran inside, wiped the beer from my face and ran back outside. The fireworks display had already resumed. Ashamed the neighbors now knew I was a "retard," I sat alone on the front lawn.

Treasures

One early morning in August, I set out on one of my many walks to look for worms, returnable bottles and new treasures. A few weeks before I had found a metal box with a snap on it and began collecting pieces of colored glass, buttons, and bits of metal; all hiding among the rubbish in the ditches. The sun was getting a later and later start and had just begun to turn the Earth a light tangerine color. Shuffling along the side of the road I felt the cold dirt under my feet. Every rock and pebble sent an electric shock through my legs. The ground was wet and the weather had turned unseasonably cold the night before. In anticipation of a move before school began all warm clothes had been packed and put in storage. My daily outfit consisted of cotton shorts and a t-shirt.

Bending to get a closer look, the shadows of the ditch moved with the sun and revealed two brand new five-dollar bills. I lumbered into the deep trench. I quickly snatched the bills and held them tightly in my hand. A sting of pain hit my foot with every step. Teetering on one leg I lifted and grabbed my ankle. There was something protruding from the bottom of my foot. Blood covered my right hand as I rooted out a piece of broken glass. I managed to keep the bills clean in my left hand.

I hobbled home as fast as I could, leaving behind bloody my footprint. I swung open the rickety wood-framed screen door. *He* was standing at the counter, scooping coffee into the pot. *He* was getting ready for work. I ran over to *him* and held out my hand. "Look! Look!"

He took a step back and raised *his* eyebrows. "Well, what have you got there?"

He was suddenly aware of the bloody footprints on the floor, "geez, are you okay?" *He* bent down lifted my foot. "Let's get that taken care of, shall we?"

Sitting at the kitchen table, *He* patched the open gash with napkins and duct tape. "All better." *He* stood me up and wrapped *his* arms around me. Long hugs meant *he* was happy and that made me happy.

"Can I keep it?" I asked. "Please?"

"No, I've got a great idea. You'll love it." *He* took the ten dollars off the table and put it in *his* pocket.

I resigned myself to the notion that *He* took the money, and I was not getting it back but it did make *him* happy. I was surprised when the next day, *he* came home and gave me a brand-new baseball glove. "Guess how much it cost?" *He* asked.

"I don't know," I shrugged.

He rolled *his* eyes and said, "come on, let's go." *He* took my hand, and we walked down the street to a park. This became our evening routine for the rest of the summer. *He* taught me how to throw and catch a baseball. When *he* was at work, I spent hours practicing. I'd throw the ball straight up as hard as I could and then run to catch it. It wasn't long before the neighborhood kids joined in and we formed entire baseball teams.

It was a great summer!

Chapter 28

A New House

The best summer had come and gone. We moved into our new house and into a new school district as well. Every other house looked like the one next to it with a slightly different shade of brick or shutters. The neighborhood was stark and void of any good sturdy trees. The trees were small and held up by rope and stakes. Our house was a small grey brick ranch. Our house was on one of only three streets that ran parallel to each other. The chances of Mimi getting lost were slim.

There was a brown version of our house just next door. The family that lived there had a little girl my age, Melanie. She was shy at first and so was I. After starting the fourth grade, I found out she was in my class, and we became friends. We spent hours in her garage playing with Barbie dolls. Her parents looked at me funny sometimes. On more than one occasion her father pulled in after work and shoo-ed us out of the way. He drove a brand new brown 1984

Buick Regal. As if taking his cue from an idyllic TV family, he'd step out of the car carrying his briefcase in one hand and keys in the other, look down at us playing and ask, "whacha got there?"

"Nothing. Just playing, Daddy," Melanie would reply.

He'd linger for a moment, shrug his shoulders, and head in the house through the garage door. In the five years we lived next door to Melanie, her parents never allowed me in their house and she never came to mine.

At the edge of our neighborhood, two streets over, there was a dense wooded area. I often found myself wondering over to the woods and making friends with the trees. A small creek ran through the woods and made it the perfect place for catching frogs and toads.

Our house was set up like a typical three-bedroom ranch. The living room was located at the front of the house, the kitchen was straight to the back. Between the living room and kitchen was a long hallway with all three bedrooms and bathroom. It only took a couple of weeks for the smell of cigarettes to cover every fabric of the house. A momentary release of fresh brewed coffee occurred every morning and sometimes in the evenings but only when company came over.

Stepmom and *His* friends often came over when *he* was working. My role was to make sure everyone had hot coffee, their cigarettes were lit, and the ashtrays promptly emptied. I tried my best to be graceful. Stepmom's newest nickname for me, Grace, was her way of letting me know how clumsy I was (no reminder was needed).

Stepmom often sent me to the basement to look for food items on the pantry shelves or the bathroom to fetch her a pill or two. Peering into the medicine cabinet at the dozen or so prescription bottles, I was never quick enough. "For heaven's sake! Have you got it yet?" Her voice struck down the hall like a lightning bolt.

"Not yet. Sorry. I can't find it." I'd call back.

"Useless." She'd snap.

Stepmom's crackling ankles came clicking down the hall. "Move," she barked.

Over the summer I had shot up at least a foot. Puberty was determined on coming early. I was all of a sudden taller and thinner, had hips and began to develop breasts. I was taller than Stepmom but still felt like an infant in her presence. She shoved me over and began rifling through the pill bottles. I never paid attention enough to know what her particular ailment was, it was simply a relief to know she would soon be passed out.

In addition to serving evening guests, us kids were responsible for cleaning the house. We rotated the living room, kitchen, and bathroom. The Princess, our stepsister, was often excused from her responsibilities and left to hang out with her friends in the evening. I didn't mind too much. My stepsister complained about everything. I enjoyed the time I spent out of my room, even if it meant dusting and running a massive vacuum. According to *Him* the vacuum was the best ever made but I'm pretty sure it was *his* justification for spending an entire month's salary. *He* also sold the monstrosities door to door for a while until *he* landed a job working afternoons in a factory.

The Naked Lady

The living room was small. Crammed within the square room was a large couch, reclining rocking chair, a China cabinet, massive television, an ashtray that weighed as much as a small elephant and a naked lady who hung in the window. The ashtray was a full green glass structure that looked like a coffee table. The only thing that adorned the glass top were hundreds of cigarette butts. A large lamp illuminated the room from the corner where it sat on an average-sized end table.

We were not permitted on the furniture. *He* thought us to be animals, *his* "Brood" he called us. We were relegated to sit on the floor. My stepsister was the exception. She was the Princess and didn't seem to be subjected to the same treatment. She was pretty. She was smart. She was thin. She was all the things the rest of us were not.

He and Stepmom were not big on watching TV. Most of the time my stepbrother and I would find ourselves in the basement trying to sneak a show or two on the 13-inch set. Watching television upstairs came with risks and a great deal of vulnerability. Sitting on the floor was a must unless we were requested to sit next to, *or on*, an adult. My spot on the floor was in the direct path of everyone who wanted to go anywhere else in the house. It was the cross-section between the living room, kitchen, and hallway.

When I became engrossed in a show, *He* would pretend to walk by but then knock me over. My back smacking the floor. *He* would quickly plant *his* feet on my hair, grab my arms and pull up as hard as *he* could. The skin on my face peeled back. *His* obnoxious laughter told me to laugh too. Yanking my arms up and then down again, I'd begin to cry.

"You're such a pussy." *He* spit. Disappointment dripped from his cracked lips.

Some nights *he* was not mean like that and would tell me to come sit next to *him*. "How do like the movie?" *he* asked.

Not knowing what to say, "oh, it's good."

His voice continued but I didn't understand *him*. I sat next to *him* and then *he* positioned me to lay across *his* lap. *His* hand rested on my side for a while. *He* began swirling *his* fingers in a circle on my stomach. My arms pinched when *he* pulled me further down the couch. Suddenly very aware of my developing body and ill-fitting nightgown, I began to shiver. I had held onto my favorite Care Bear nightgown, the one with purple on the sleeves. *His* hand didn't have to move far when *he* put it inside my nightgown. *His* finger continued to swirl on my stomach. I felt *his* hand move down farther and farther. Claiming health reasons, we were not permitted to wear underwear and *his* hand went inside. *He* was gentle and slow and spoke softly. I did what I supposed to do, nothing. *Don't move. Don't breathe. Don't speak. He'll be done soon.*

I watched my body move and exhale. I laid half on *his* lap and my head and shoulders on the next cushion as I watched the television screen. The credits began to roll, and I started to inch away. *He* swept my legs around. I got up and began walking to bed. I had reached the hallway and *he* said, "hey, come here. Aren't you going to give me a kiss goodnight?"

Without hesitation I turned around and headed back to *him*. *He* already did what *he* usually did, the danger was over. I reached the couch, leaned over and *he* pulled me in tight. *He* was hugging me. It was warm and comforting. I melted into *his* large chest. A rush of pain and pressure jolted me from my relaxed state. All the air left my body and I forgot how to breathe. Gripping the ornate wood trim that lined the back of the couch, I watched the naked lady. The way she danced in her rainforest. I listened to her humming with the falling rain. The oil sliding down the bars. Did she know she was in prison? She looks so sensual and peaceful with her hands on her head and breasts. Was she proud? The oil glistened from the lamp as it swung front to back, back to front; no more.

I stood up, no longer a little girl of ten-years-old. I pulled at my nightgown. I was again woefully aware of how short it had been, *no more. I won't wear this one anymore*, I thought. *He's watching*.

"Walk," Anna whispered. "Walk."

It didn't happened, my mind repeated, *it didn't happened*.

I turned and said, "goodnight."

"Goodnight." *His* voice was sturdy. *He* was unchanged.

Anna With V

"It was a trick," Anna said.

"What was?" V asked.

"He tricked me. He didn't want a hug, did he?"

Surprised by her naivety, V replied, "yes, it was a trick. *He* didn't love you. What *he* did is not love."

"I am so sorry Anna. *He* should have never done that." V said.

Anna sat up and looked at her picture on the family diagram.

Anna's memories fade from one event to another. She is naive and vulnerable, and every trick feels like the first time.

"Can you tell me any other times when he tricked you?" V's soft voice lingered in the office.

Anna's head fell. She took a pen and piece of paper off the long coffee table in front of them and began to draw. A small table. A large bed. Four long posts reaching up to the ceiling. A small window. Another small table. A large dresser.

"I was sleeping," Anna whispered.

"In his room?" V asked.

"Yeah. *He* gave me lunch and told me to lay down in *his* room. I was tired."

"How old were you?"

"I'm ten," Anna said. Confused by the question, she sat up straight and furrowed her eyebrows.

"Oh, yes, I see." V glanced at the clock and asked, "What happened next?"

Anna began to draw again. A figure appeared on the bed, then two figures.

"I was sleeping." Anna began to shake and cry. "He's right there," pointing at the second figure wrapped around the first.

"It's grey out there." Anna's voice flattened.

"Out where?"

"Outside. See the window?" Anna gestured to the window in the picture. Her finger remained on the picture. Eyes wide and staring at nothing, she left herself. As if stuck in an old painting, her body remained affixed in this position for several more minutes.

Anna was with *Him* now. *Him* under the covers, behind her. She slipped out the window.

It's so grey outside, Anna thought.

Jolts of pain brought her back to *Him*, back to the blinking alarm clock on the end table in *his* bedroom. It read 12:11 PM. She couldn't move under the heavy brown comforter. *He* had her. *Not there! Not there!* She screamed it in her head. Her hands gripped the edge of bed.

"You're okay," *he* said. "You're okay. Say it. Say, I'm okay." *His* voice was stern.

The smell of *his* breath wafted across her face, cigarettes and the faint smell of the bologna sandwiches they had eaten for lunch. *He* pulled her closer.

Anna whimpered, "I'm okay. I'm okay. I'm okay."

It's so grey outside, Anna thought. *I'm okay. I'm okay. I'm okay.*

"Anna?" V asked. Anna remained stoic and immovable. "Anna?"

"Anna, come here with me now," V said.

Anna looked around, still without emotion, she was back with V.

"I'm here. Sorry. It's okay. I'm okay." Anna came alive with a sudden realization.

V pulled Anna close. "You're here now. *He's* not here. You're here now."

V's words softened Anna. Tears fell.

Anna looked at V and said, "Maybe *he* didn't mean to do those things. Maybe *he* can't help it. *He* liked me sometimes."

"When did *he* like you?"

"*He* shared *his* math books with me. I'm good at math. *He* asked me to make *his* dinner a lot. *He* says I'm the only one *he* can count on to not tell." Anna began rubbing her hands together. "But I am telling. *He's* going to find me and then we'll all be in trouble."

V took Anna's hands in hers and said, "*He's* not looking for you."

V took out a small note card and wrote, "*He's* not looking for me."

"Put this where you can see it every day." V handed the small note to Anna. I took the note and put in my pocket. Anna had slipped out of the room and out of my mind.

I looked at V.

"Welcome back," V said.

Chapter 29

Journal Entry from Anna – November 25, 2017

I know stuff she doesn't know, and I can tell things that Amy won't. I know who we are, and she still won't let us be who we are, always trying to pretend that we are imaginary and wrong and made up. We are real. I am real. And I know stuff.

I'm the only one that protect Mimi. I'm the only one who can hold her, well, sometimes Mommy but not all the time. I'm the only one who knows. Sometimes I think there are more of us, and they are going to tell, no matter what. It's all a big secret. We hold secrets too but only if they don't seem real or right or fit. I am not a liar. I am here for Mimi, and I take over when nobody else can be quiet and take in the pain. The pain, Mimi, and V belong to me.

Why do I feel this way? So needy. So sad. So weak and scared. I want to be with V all the time. I know it's the little ones, Mimi and Six, but I'm little too. I'm going to wear her out. She won't love me anymore. I ask for too much. Everyone goes away. I can't love too much; she'll go away too. Is this what it feels like to be loved? I'm so sad it's taken this long to feel it. So afraid she'll leave us. We won't survive it; I'll make sure of it.

V's Angel

I got to V's office early and figured she would be late. V usually ran a few minutes behind and I a few minutes early. I passed the time by turning on the lights, setting the thermostat, and pacing from room to room. The main floor is comprised of an entry way with two doors, a waiting room, a small toddler playroom and my personal favorite, the sand tray room. I'm still not sure how, but I talked V into letting me paint a giant mural on all four walls. It was the best work I have done so far, and the biggest canvas I've ever worked with.

I spent time planning and sketching the perfect sunrise over the mountains. I painted a waterfall that took up half of one wall, which I had made the spring wall. Each wall transitioned into a season. My favorite was where Autumn transitions into Winter. The red and orange hues of the Autumn sky become rich Evergreens and stark white snow. Visiting the mural, I ran my hand along a single deer set against white mountains. The moon, far bigger and brighter than an average moon appears enchanting against the crisp navy-blue sky. Behind the finely detailed mountains I could imagine a tiny village hidden away from all the stresses of the daily grind.

I like arriving early and having a few moments to wave at the familiar creatures I have created. The bunny greets me at the door. I often slide my hand to the next wall and stroke the bird perched on a tree in the summer. As Autumn approaches, a chipmunk pokes his head out from behind large maple tree.

The sand table sits in the center of the room and the mural surrounds it. Using various toys and objects, we use the sand table to create room and villages. It's where odd stories emerge and hearts are healed. Okay, maybe that's a bit too much. It's where we play.

Not long before, around Christmas time, Anna had picked out a special gift for V. We were at the local store and spotted a beautiful little ceramic angel. I had been coming to grips more and more with the fact that the little ones on the family diagram were me but not me. They were their own people. They had their own experiences and memories and together, with V, my life was beginning to make sense. I felt more than gratitude for V's love and acceptance of us, even when I didn't love or accept us. Anna and I wanted to get something special for V for Christmas.

I saw a sweet ceramic angel and though maybe this was the gift we would get V. Anna and I had collaborated on what kind of gift was appropriate but none of that mattered when Mimi chimed in and said, "get it." I picked it up. I circled the store once more and decided to go back to get one more. One for V and one for us to keep at home. We wanted to see her every day, even if it was in the shape of a tiny angel. We took both of the little ceramic angels home. Anna drew two little hearts on the bottom, one heart for from Anna and one heart from little Mimi.

The day I brought V her angel, I had already set our angel on the little bookshelf in my living room. V placed her angel on her desk. She said, "I think this fits perfect right here." Her eyes brightened and softly smiled at Anna and Mimi. It *was* the perfect place.

A few weeks later while visiting the animals in the mural, I noticed the angel in the sand tray room. It was in the wrong place, and it was broken.

My heart sank at the sight of the angel with a missing head. The head was sitting next to it and I quickly gathered my emotions and thought, *it's an accident, it's fine. I'll bring some glue next week and fix it.*

"No, it's not okay," Anna said. "She doesn't care. Why is it down here? She doesn't care."

Anna took the angel's body and head and sat on the floor.

We heard V's car pull into the parking lot. *This looks weird,* I thought. Anna and I had been holding the same headspace for too long. One of us had to go away, at least for a little while. I carefully stood up and placed the angel and her head back on the shelf and went into the therapy room.

The session was benign and stale. I could not get Anna to stop being sad but I was too embarrassed to tell V how upset she was over a silly little ceramic angel.

The following week, I brought in the super glue. To my great surprise I did not have the time to grab the angel and secretly fix it. V, uncharacteristically, had showed up ten minutes early. I decided to leave the angel broken until next time I was alone in V's office. I didn't want her to think it bothered me or Anna.

V and I entered her therapy room. I sat down on the loveseat. Anna's sadness weighed on me. I excused myself and said, "I have to do this." I retrieved the angel from the sand tray room. After placing her on the coffee table, I pulled some super glue from my purse. I gently held the little angel body in one hand and her tiny head in the other and glued the two together. "Sorry, I noticed her in the other room and I have to fix it."

I am still not sure of V's exact words but something about someone used in a therapy session and got upset and broke the angel. Anna's heart sank. The thought of someone else touching the angel welled up as anger and jealousy but also fear. She couldn't let V know how she felt. The thought of V angry or upset was too much. It would ruin everything.

My head became fuzzy. Anna and I struggled inside for control.

"Tell her!" Anna cried.

"No, it's okay. It was a gift, she can do what she wants with it," I piped back.

"It was from us. She doesn't care."

"No. It's fine." My reassurance did not sway Anna, it only pushed me farther back.

Ann won. I could not hold her back anymore.

"Will you take it home, V?" Anna asked.

"What?" V asked. She was unaware of the events that have led to this moment.

"The angel," Anna whimpered.

V's face suddenly changed as she exclaimed, "oh my gosh, I am so sorry." V pulled Anna in close as Anna began to sob. "I am so sorry. It was careless of me. Do you forgive me?"

"Yeah, I'm sorry. It's okay." Anna's voice was shaky and small. Her heart settled and melted into V's arms.

The following session, V took a picture of the angel in V's favorite workspace at home. This was more assurance of V's love for Anna and Mimi. More than just a little ceramic angel had been broken and mended in those moments. We were whole again.

Email from Me to V – February 24, 2019

Nothing rips apart the soul like sexual abuse. The shame, guilt, fear, and rage. It permeates in ways that all other offenses pale in comparison. We cannot build a beautiful new self on a shitty shame-filled, broken foundation. We are dismantling it from the bottom up, cleaning each piece, making it shiny and new and placing it back into the soul, the heart, with new purpose, new hope, and new light.

Today, that is what this feels like, through our relationship with you and all of the parts. Today, I see it, I feel it, and know that even the crappiest days can have meaning and purpose.

Chapter 30

Me and Jacob

Fifth grade brought about many changes, changes in my body and in our home. My older sister got kicked out the house, and the older nieces and friends of friends had come and gone. A few children remained. I played with my stepbrother, Jacob, the most.

Jacob was small for his age and sported the same flaming red hair and small facial features as his mother. He was usually the punching bag for the adults in the house. The other kids in the house never bothered us too much. Due to our outcast positions, Jacob and I got along well.

While doing laundry in the basement Jacob and I got curious about some boxes that had not been unpacked from our move the year before. We had found an old broken radio and decided we could fix it. Excited for our new adventure, we folded the pile of clothes, one of our chores for the day, and quietly snuck out to the garage. There we found tiny screwdrivers and an old rusty switchblade.

Jacob and I weren't sure where to go to work on our new project.

"Can we go to your room?" Jacob asked. "No, *He* checks in all the time. We'll have to go to your room." Jacob nodded in agreement, and we carefully placed the tools in our pants pockets.

Forgetting ourselves, Jacob and I closed the door and began to work on the radio. We were not permitted to close doors, otherwise *Him* and Stepmom assumed we had entered into some kind of conspiratorial planning to ruin the family.

He was only home for another hour before *he* had to go to work. *He* was preoccupied with taking a shower and getting ready. Jacob and I figured we could play undetected. We pulled out the tools we had retrieved from the garage, took the back panel off the radio, and slowly began to disassemble it. We pushed and twisted and turned our tools on small tabs and nodules inside. Excited to see if our tinkering had worked, I plugged in the radio and checked the dials.

Static!

Wide-eyed and grinning Jacob and I looked at each other.

"Oh my God!" We both squealed.

The door then swung open. *He* stood there. *His* eyes darted at the radio and then to me, then to Jacob.

"Who said you could you play in here?"

"No one," Jacob whispered.

My lips wouldn't move. I wanted to tell *him* we had fixed the radio. I wanted to tell *him* we would put it back together. No words came out.

Already hunched over the bed as we worked on the radio, we didn't move very far. *He* told us to take off our clothes. In typical fashion, my voice returned with loud shrieks.

"I didn't mean to!" I screamed.

That never worked. I heard my voice from a distance and thought, *stop saying that!* As *his* belt swung, Jacob and I cried and screamed but it only worsened the punishment. Stepmom leaned against the doorframe and looked down at us. She held a lit cigarette in one hand and a glass of Bourbon in the other. When H*e* was done with us, I retreated to my room. Jacob and I never attempted to play with the radio, explore electronics, or play with *his* tools again. We were unsure of which infraction had caused the punishment.

"Hey," Jacob's voice crackled.

I picked up the walkie-talkie. *He* didn't know Grandma had given me walkie-talkies for my birthday.

"*He* went to work. It's okay now," I said.

"Can I come in?" Jacob sniffled. He was still crying from the beating. He always got twice as much as the rest of us. He was a boy and according to *Him*, was weak. "I'll turn you into a man yet!" *He* would scream at Jacob.

It wasn't Jacob's fault he was so little. His

small stature came in handy when we retreated to my closet. It was another hiding place that *Him* and Stepmom could never reach.

"Come on, come over," I said over the walkie.

A few minutes later Jacob entered my room. I left the door open just a crack.

"We need to hear if your mom is coming," I said.

Jacob carried his favorite stuffed lion. We opened my closet door. Bookshelves lined the entire back wall of the closet and made the perfect ladder for reaching our hideout. Jacob went first. He reached the top of the shelves, put his hands on the ceiling and moved over a small hatch to the attic. I passed him the lion, my Care Bear, and a flashlight.

Though not as graceful, I quickly followed Jacob up the shelves and into the attic. The rafters pressed down on our backs as we sat and played pretend with our stuffed animals. We stashed ramen noodles and Mad Lib magazines. We spent hours in the attic making up funny words for the magazine. If we missed dinner, we sucked on the ramen noodles until they were soft enough to swallow.

This night, there was no escape from Stepmom. *He* had already left for work, but she refused to be finished with us. She wasn't always mean, but the following year brought changes. After my sister left, I became the new target for Stepmom. From mismatching socks to rolling my eyes, I could do nothing right.

Over the next few years things changed. The sound of her clicking ankles gave warning to move out of range. Moving swiftly down the hallway, her long, green plush robe touched the top of her boney feet. Her thin skin exposed all the veins in her feet, as if they had been frozen and the clicking was the sound of cracking ice. The best chance for escape was the attic or basement. Her mood was unavoidable.

"Amy," her voice was loud and craggy. She called from the kitchen.

I showed no emotion as I made my way down from the attic. I reached the hallway, peaked my head around the corner and said, "yeah?"

"What the hell is this?"

"I don't know."

"Look. Look. Get your ass over here and look." She met me in the hallway and grabbed my arm. She pulled me into the kitchen and positioned me in front of the long counter. All thoughts left me, my legs stood straight, and I stared at her small pale green eyes.

There was no time to react, she turned me around, grabbed my head and pressed my face to the counter. I had missed the crumbs under the toaster, a grave mistake in a house that was meant to be immaculate. It wasn't my day to clean the kitchen. Her precious Princess had gotten out of her chores again.

"Stupid!" Stepmom said.

Stepmom glared at me. I lifted my head, and she caught me rolling my eyes. Yet another infraction to be followed with a good smack to my face. I straightened, giving no sign of the anger that grew within me. *Fuck her*, I thought, *FUCK her*!

Chapter 31

Shadows

The basement in the new house was much nicer than the first house. Stripped red and brown carpet covered most of the basement. Concrete floors were left exposed in the laundry room, a part of the basement that had been walled off from the rest. The walls were cold but covered in vertical dark wood paneling. Going down the basement stairs was always a bit scary. I couldn't see beyond what was at the bottom. To the right of the stairs was a large open area with a television and pullout couch.

For a while, when Stepmom and her kids were still there, I was moved to the basement because according to *Him*, Jacob and I talked too much. Our bedrooms were next to each other and if we couldn't reach each other on the walkie talkies, we spoke to each other through the heat vents on the floor.

The far end of the basement wrapped around

the corner to the right and there was a small cove, big enough for my bed and a small table. My room had one lamp that sat on the side table, but it required navigating my way through the dark to get to it. The main part of the basement had one overhead lamp, but the light didn't bend around the corner. There was no bedroom door to create an actual division between my room and the rest of the basement.

I didn't spend much time in my new room. But while I was doing laundry, watching tv, or attempting to get homework done, I often heard a woman call my name. "Amy," an ethereal voice cut through the silence. "Yeah?" I'd call out. There was never an answer. I often left my bed or activity in search of the voice calling my name. After several months of this and finding no one in the basement, I did my best to ignore it.

One night, I remember being completely exhausted. I had gone to school, and it was my day to clean the living room. This only consisted of vacuuming and dusting, but in typical fashion, my need to please allowed Princess to convince me that I should do her chores. It felt good when was she was nice to me, and she was nice to me when I did her favors. With a smile she said, "maybe next time I go skating, you can come." I half knew it was a lie and half hoped she was telling the truth.

Princess was a teen model and sometimes that was easier for me. I was the ugly dumb one, the one without a real name. Sitting on *his* lap, giving *him* kisses in public, and getting pats on the butt were reserved for the pretty ones. Those moments came for us when it was quiet and dark. Princess had *him* wrapped around her little finger. Princess was pretty, popular, and loved.

I spent that day cleaning the entire house and cooking spaghetti. I didn't bother to change into a nightgown for bed. I went to the basement, got under the covers and quickly fell asleep.

A sudden jolt of electricity surged through my body. I opened my eyes and saw a black mass floating at the foot of my bed. It hovered with no discernable face or legs. Draped in black flowing material it lingered for what felt like several minutes. I couldn't move. I couldn't speak or scream for help. Frozen in fear, I felt the bed fill with urine.

The voice calling my name stopped at after a few years. The shadows have stayed with me. They appear in corners and doorways. Sometimes they watch. Sometimes they don't seem to know where they are and float by quickly. The watching shadow is usually by herself. The others come in pairs or threes.

Chapter 32

Iggy with V

"He calls me Ignoramus. I know that's not my name. You can call me Iggy. *He* thinks I'm a stupid and dumb, a worthless girl. *He* asks me the weirdest questions. Things like, "what's the square root of 6,782?" I don't know anyone who knows the answers to things like that. Sometimes I do know things but can't speak. Words don't come out. They get stuck in my head and all I do is look at *Him*. I suppose I do seem dumb or retarded. I'm just a girl, I guess."

Iggy looked at V.

"I can hear you when you talk to them. Not every time but sometimes. I slip behind and listen. I can hear their voices. I can hear their stories. They love you." Iggy's voice softened and she picked Anna's picture up from the family diagram.

"The younger ones call you Mommy, you

know. Anna won't say it, but she calls you Mommy too. It doesn't matter I suppose, everyone wants a mother."

Iggy kept her gaze on Anna's photo.

"I don't have a mother," Iggy whispered and slowly put the picture back on the posterboard.

V gently took Iggy's hand and asked, "How did you come to be with Amy?"

"I was in the truck."

"What truck?" V asked.

"It was Amy's truck. We were eleven years old; I think. I can show Amy and she will have to tell you. Is that okay?" Iggy asked.

"Yes, of course," said V.

For the next hour me and Iggy told V about the truck, and *Him*.

The Truck

The summer I turned eleven years old was a relief. It was the first summer without Stepmom and Princess, but I did miss Jacob. It was a good summer. Most days I rode my bike, roller skated or walked in the woods near my house.

He slept most of the day and went to work around 4 PM. I spent another hour or so riding my bike or doing whatever activity I could, outside of the house, until I was sure *he* had gone. *He* came home around midnight. The time in between *his* departure for work and *his* return was spent eating as much as I could find, sometimes throwing it up and drinking vodka. The vodka was kept in supply at the bottom of the pantry. Both *he* and I pretended the bottles were not getting more and more empty. When the vodka had reached a critical low point, usually an inch or two at the bottom of the gallon jug, a new one would appear. A small glass was all I needed to pass out most nights. If I kept myself just drunk enough, *His* coming home was only a brief interruption, and I could still function the next day.

One day in July, I had rolled up into the driveway after a long bike ride. There was a pick-up truck parked where *his* minivan was normally parked. The front was low to the ground and painted a dull grey. Spray paint had been used to try and cover the pockets of rust on the doors and hood. The back of the truck was a large wooden shed-type structure. Looking like a doghouse for an oversized red cartoon dog, the truck was hideous. The wood structure was bare, had a small window on the driver's side, and a door with a lock on the back.

"Um, what is that?" I asked as *He* was coming out of the garage. It was early evening. *He is supposed to be at work,* I thought. It suddenly occurred to me that it was a Sunday, I had miscalculated but it was too late, I was now home. *He* had a dirty rag in *his* hands and was wiping off some oil. *He* was never much of a mechanic, the whole scene felt strange.

"It's a truck, Ignoramus." *He* rolled *his* eyes and chuckled.

I knew it was a truck. "Why's it here?" I asked.

"I got it for you."

He grinned wide, revealing his crooked yellow teeth.

"Don't you like it? It's for you."

I didn't understand. I was still years away from getting my license. *Was he going to let me drive it before I got my license? He* let me steer the car when I was little, and *he* wasn't one for following the rules. Maybe it *was* for me. I didn't press any further. *His* eyes darted my way almost begging for a bigger conversation. I laid my bike on the lawn and walked to the front door.

"Hey!" *He* yelled. "Get over here and check it out."

I began walking toward the truck. *He* met me halfway and grabbed my arm.

"Here. Get in."

We walked to the back of the truck. *He* unlocked the padlock and the small wooden door swung open. I stepped back.

"Come on. What the hell is wrong with you?" *He* asked.

He softened for a moment and gently motioned to the door, "I'll get pizza for dinner. Come on, check it out."

I reached over and pulled myself up to the door, *He* was behind me. I stumbled in and onto floor of the odd wooden shed. A thick black sleeping bag covered most of the floor. I thought, *He must have bought it for camping*. No way was this for me.

The smell of cedar and stale cigarette smoke permeated every corner. The window was situated high on the left side with a large nail next to it. I had seen that large nail trick before, in the basement, in the kitchen, in *His* room. I wondered what kind of belt *he'd* hang on this one. The truck *was* for me. Hunched over, I slowly began to back up.

"I can't even stand up here," I yelled out to *him*.

I turned to find *him* close behind me. *He* was blocking my only exit. Time passed. I watched the sun set through the only window. *His* breath on me.

His sweat on me.

"It's okay," *he* said in my ear. "You can handle it."

All emotion drained from my body and mind. Iggy took over.

"I can handle it," Iggy repeated. "It's okay, I'm okay."

The night went on as usual. I rubbed *his* feet and made us dinner. *He* never ordered the pizza *he* promised, it was just another trick.

Me with V

I sat in V's office and stared at the thirteen pictures posted to the family diagram. A diagram created to explore each little girl that shared experiences with *Him*. Little by little, week by week, I began to see me in some of the photos. I recognized the other people, places, and remembered being at the events where the photo was taken but still, they were not me.

"I know that's me in the picture but she's not me," I picked up the picture of Anna and then Iggy, "and she's not me."

"They are." V was steady and quick in her response, "But they are also separate. You share one body, but I understand that they are not you. You feel what they feel. You hear what they hear. You survived because they were created. You survived because God created your mind to protect you from the horrible things that were happening to you."

I looked out the window through a small crack

in the blinds. I felt myself slip back behind a veil. V's
voice was in the distance. I was unsure of which little
one had taken over. Our head pressed against V's
chest. *I can hear her heartbeat*, a young voice
resounded in my head. Our breathing slowed to match
V's as she read the story out loud.

Chapter 33

Journal Entry from Me to V – February 24, 2018

My head is so fuzzy today. I know things aren't right. I don't know who I am sometimes or why my body feels the way it does. Flashes of memory, or dream maybe? I am so unsure anymore. You are not unsure. Mimi calls you Mommy and the other littles too, but they won't say it out loud. Six still waits to see if it's safe and Anna grows more and more skeptical that anyone could love such a gross, unwanted, sad little girl; maybe it is all a trick.

The first sign of abandonment and Anna is building up her walls, bracing for the worst. I suppose it doesn't matter too much anymore. We've seen enough, been through enough, and are smart enough to know that nothing is forever, nothing is consistent for long, and all of the love and warmth experienced in a moment, deepens the sadness. We know moments will come when things stop being what they are. People stop loving, hugging, or even breathing. We brace ourselves for those moments.

Holding tight to the pieces of the walls we have built,
so the next sign of abandonment, we can rebuild.
Problem is, each time we build with our pieces of
wall, they become more worn, broken, and crinkled.
Each time we build, our walls are thinner and more
cracked than the time before. Like ripping up
cardboard and then trying to tape it all back together,
over and over again.

Our walls are thin, emotions creep in and we
are tired. We are sad. We are vulnerable. These are
not things we are used to; it's been too long since
we've experienced real emotions. I think perhaps
some of us haven't experienced many emotions. The
only emotions felt when we were young was fear and
neediness. Our misguided sense of loyalty stops us
even now from feeling what we should or could.
Trying to protect Him, seems like the only way to
protect us. We relive it and relive it and relive it, until
it is limp and stale. What then? Who are we without
our fear and loyalty? Who are we if not the servants
rebuilding the wall? Who are we if not the
gatekeepers, the trauma-holders, the littles? When all
the trauma has been weeded through, when all of the
emotions have been unleashed and washed out, when
the littles no longer see themselves as little, who are
we? Alone.

Chapter 34

Everyone is Gone

When I was in the seventh grade, Stepmom moved out and took her kids with her. I was alone. To some degree, I was free. I was free from a watchful eye when *He* wasn't home. I was free from getting in trouble for random errors. I was free from watching Princess steal all of *his* time during the day. I was free from padlocks on the refrigerator and reminder notes of how fat I was posted to the pantry door. I was free from pouring her coffee. I was free from the sound of her coming down the hall, the sight of her fuzzy robe, her yellow teeth, and the sting of her hand across my face. Yep, I was free.

I missed Jacob. He was my friend, my brother and my only ally. I had left for school one morning and came home to find them all gone. All but *Him*. *He* continued to work afternoons, so all was not lost. *He* still had all of my nights, but I would have most of the day and my afternoons to do what I wanted.

On the weekends and the time between school

and *Him* going to work, I needed to find something to do. I also needed to find a way to buy my own food. *He* rarely went grocery shopping and when *he* did, we ended with spaghetti, bologna, lemonade, and ramen noodles.

I had a few friends at school with baby-sitting jobs and thought I could probably get a job too. Babies were terrifying. I wanted to work and make money, but I was not about to watch babies or even kids younger than me. I still found comfort in my evening drinking and figured no parent would allow that around their children. I was not about to give up my vodka.

Tired of being hungry. Tired of waiting on *Him* to buy food. Tired of eating instant noodles and bologna. I needed a job.

One afternoon, I returned home from school. The bus took me to the intersection at the end of our long street. Getting off the bus, I looked for my neighbor, Melanie, but she wasn't there. I walked home along. My mind raced with the possibility that *He* was there and awake.

After a slow walk home, I picked up the

newspaper from the porch and went in the house. The squeal from me opening the door was unavoidable. *He* always knew when I came home.

"What took you so long?" Looking at *his* watch, *he* raised *his* brows and peered over the top of *his* glasses.

"The bus was late," I stated.

He stood in the middle of the kitchen and nodded *his* head toward the sink. I was well aware of my kitchen duties. There weren't that many dishes. It was just *him* and I now. All of the chores now belonged to me. I cooked. I cleaned. I gave *him* hugs and rubbed *his* feet. It was me *he* would talk to about *his* 'ignorant' coworkers. It was me *he* depended on to make sure everything was immaculate. Most days I was happy to oblige. Most days, *he* was pleased with my performance.

A performance, yes, that's what it was. A movie with no production team, no stage, no audience, but a performance was right. I didn't ask questions. I simply took direction. I didn't try to save myself. I didn't know I needed rescuing. I didn't reject *his* advances. I didn't struggle when *he* visited my room. I didn't yet know *he* wasn't supposed to do that. *He* quoted Bible verses to make sure I knew that God told *him* it was right. I was to obey and be quiet and above all, "honor my father."

"Family business is family business," *he* said every morning. We were never permitted to talk about anything that happened at home, not with outsiders and not with each other.

Work

As a kid I was always resourceful. For better or worse, I did what I needed to do to survive. I stole food in elementary school. I created forts and hiding places in every home we lived. I escaped into the trees when my mind left, and my body stayed. I would always find a way to survive.

At twelve years old, I needed and wanted a job. I didn't want to depend on *him* to bring home the same nasty food. I needed an excuse to not be home. In the early 1980s, it wasn't so unheard of to have a job at twelve years old.

One morning I walked to the local stores and restaurants. There was a one strip mall about a mile from my house. I started at the convenient store.

"Sir, do you have any positions available?" I was a tall, sturdy girl and used to hard work. "Like, sweeping or cleaning or anything?"

"No, sorry."

I left the corner store feeling a little defeated. I wanted to work there because they had everything. They sold pop and chips and cigarettes. If I couldn't work there, I wouldn't be able to steal the cigarettes. Stealing *His* were not an option anymore. *He* had caught on to my thievery and kept *his* cigarettes in *his* front shirt pocket. I had kept the last note from Stepmom when she used to send me to the store to buy her cigarettes. Nobody knew she didn't live there anymore but the note was getting ragged, and the store clerk was beginning to question its legitimacy.

I went next door to the Mexican restaurant. I could smell the fresh taco and tostado shells. Red and green plastic peppers swung from the ceiling. The Virgin Mary greeted me at the cash register. A giant statue, she stood at least four feet tall. My church days had been spent learning about fundamental Baptist teachings and a constant reminder that the Virgin Mary should not be idolized. There was constant condemnation of the Catholic faith in my church. I didn't quite understand it, but I wasn't taught to question anything.

A woman came through the swinging door between the kitchen and dining room. Wavy jet-black hair that hung to her waist and swayed in the opposite direction of her hips. Her wide smile made her eyes almost disappear into two coin-slots. Tiny bells rang from around the bottom of her bright red and blue dress.

"Ola dear," she said.

She was out of breath but seemed pleased to see me. It was 11:00 AM on a Saturday and the place was empty.

"Do you have any jobs I could do?" I asked.

I began fidgeting with the head of baby Jesus in front of me.

"Well, let's see."

Her smiled faded as she looked around the restaurant and then back at me.

"Do you know how to cook?" she asked.

"Oh, yes," I said.

I knew how to cook pasta and heat things up,

but I had never tried cooking Mexican food.

"Can you clean?"

I nodded yes.

"You start tomorrow."

"Thank you!" I said and bolted out the door. I could hardly contain myself but managed to get outside before realizing I hadn't asked her what time. I ran back in and before I could say anything, she screamed from the swinging door, "TOMORROW! TWO O'CLOCK!"

My walk home was light and quick. I had a job. My first job.

For the next four months I worked at Minnie's Mexican Lindo. I cooked all kinds of foods. I cleaned dishes and mopped floors. I got to eat dinner every night and the best part; I was getting paid, sort of. About three weeks after working at Minnie's, I received my first paycheck. Sixty dollars!

It was official, I was now part of the working

class. My paycheck came in a fancy envelope. One major problem quickly struck me. How do I get money from this? I had never been into a bank. I didn't have a bank account. I was going to have to ask *Him* for help.

He agreed to help me open an account and deposit the money. I didn't want to deposit anything. I wanted the cash. We drove to the bank, and *he* told me to sign the back of my check.

He looked over at me and said, "Let's go start a college fund for you."

I was very confused. *He* had told me for years I was dumb. I couldn't learn and should marry a man who would take care of me. According to *him*, I was not college material. I knew then my job wasn't for me at all. I couldn't bear to quit the job that fed me, kept from being home, and provided me with people to talk to. *He* took every penny of my paychecks. I *was* stupid. Sometime just after Christmas, I walked to work and found a note on the door that Minnie's had permanently closed. I was devasted but vowed to find a job that would pay me cash.

Chapter 35

Thirteen-years-old

My eight-grade year was filled with friends, dances, and art. Despite my continued and consistent drinking in the evening, I found new confidence at school. My teachers like me. I did well in my academic and creative courses. My ego grew that year, along with the size of breasts. I started wearing make-up and miniskirts. At the beginning of the school year, my friend, Nikki introduced me to her boyfriend's friend. His name was Cori. He was a senior and I was eager to prove my position in my friend group. The four of us, me, Nikki, Cori, and Nikki's boyfriend often spent our afternoons and sometimes evenings hanging out in the trailer park where Cori lived with his dad.

Cori didn't stand a chance. I knew what guys wanted and I gave it to him. When *He* found about my boyfriend, *he* grounded me. I didn't give a shit anymore. I was going to get in trouble regardless of

what I did or did not do, *might as well have fun*, I
thought.

I began sneaking out through my window
after *He* got from work and did what *he* wanted with
me. It was usually 3 or 4 AM when I'd slide open my
window and plop down into a large barberry bush. I
let *Him* do whatever *he* wanted without complaint.
Sometimes I volunteered, knowing I would meet up
with Cori later that night. I did what I wanted to do. I
did what I *had* to do. I do believe I loved Cori but not
in a way that kept me fawning over him. He enlisted
in the Army and immediately after my eight-grade
year, he left. I never heard from him again.

I began to grow angry and resentful that year.
I was tired of *Him*. I had spent enough time with my
friends that I began to understand maybe fathers were
not supposed to do those things with their daughters.

At night, *He* entered my room, sometimes
under the guise that I had a fever. I was often drowsy
from the vodka I had drank a couple of hours before
he came home from work. *He* regularly sat softly on
the side of my bed, touched my forehead and said,
"you have a fever. You must be sick. Come on." *He*
would instruct me to get undressed. "Fevers can kill
you, you know."

Together, *him* and I walked down the hall.
Him behind me. I tried to cover my nakedness. My
body shook, whether from actual fever or temperature
in the house, it made no difference. I walked over to
the counter where the medicine had already been
poured into a small cup and I drank it.

Our usual routine took us to the bathroom
where my knees became worn and my body tired. The
nights were always so dark. The tiny window in the
bathroom made me feel as if I was floating in outer
space. There was nothing else. *Him* and I. Painful.
Shameful. Alone.

Despite *His* attempts to keep me all to *himself,*
I gained useful independence in middle school.
Summer had arrived and I got my second job. This
time, instead of going on foot, I looked in the Help
Wanted section of the newspaper.

Chapter 36

Student Help Wanted for the Summer!

The headline of the advertisement read, "Student Help Wanted for the Summer!" *A perfect fit*, I thought. I was a student, and I needed a summer job. I called the phone number listed.

A woman with a sweet, calm voice answered the phone. She introduced herself as Trudy.

"Hi, yeah, I'm calling about the ad for the job," I said.

"Wonderful!" Trudy's said.

Trudy asked my name and where I lived and then told me they would pick me up the next morning.

"Super cool," I said, and hung up the phone.

The next morning, a large black passenger van pulled up to the curb in front of my house. A young man, he was maybe in his early twenties, got out of the driver's side and opened the side door. He was tall and thin. His skin was pale, and his hair was dark and greasy. I slowly walked toward the van. I was hesitant and thought about retreat until I saw an older woman in the passenger seat.

The woman rolled down the window and stuck her head out. "Hi hon. I'm Trudy. We talked yesterday. That's John." Trudy pointed at the young man holding open the side door. I smiled and walked to the van.

Sitting inside the van, were ten children. Seemingly curious, twenty eyes stared at me. There was an equal number of both boys and girls ranging from about eight years old to fourteen. I spotted a girl about my age. I stepped up into the van and sat next to her.

I was the last stop on what became the new morning routine for the crew. That day I found out I would be spending the next several weeks going door to door selling candy for a dollar. Trudy promised I would earn fifty cents for every item I sold, and I would be paid in cash!

My mornings that summer began at 8:00 AM. Most days there were 12 children picked up. We were then driven to wealthy neighborhoods and dropped off two by two at the end of the street. Trudy and John would pick us up at the other end and then take us to the next street. I usually did my runs with my new friend Melissa. She was a few months older than me and had started working with Trudy and John at the beginning of the summer.

At the end of every afternoon, the drop-off routine would end at my house. After a couple weeks, Trudy said, "Hey, I could use your help if you're interested?" She explained that she was horrible at math and needed help counting the money. I agreed. She thought I was smart, and I was eager to assist in any way I could.

The day Trudy explained she needed help, John drove a different vehicle and Melissa did not get dropped off. Trudy drove me and Melissa to the Chesterfield Motor Inn, a run-down motel situated on the corner of a busy intersection. It was there that Melissa and I were introduced to Trudy's boyfriend. He was a massive man. He was tall and his muscles were visible through his large black leather jacket. He didn't say anything to us. He scanned Melissa from top to bottom. Melissa was a short and thin girl with long curly brown hair. The kind of girl that should be on the cheer team, not hustling door to door to sell candy. Done with her, he turned his attention to me and gave a lingering stare. I felt sweat drip down the back of my neck.

Trudy put her hand on my back and led me further into the motel room. Trudy's boyfriend led us to the bed. Melissa and I cautiously sat down. Trudy pulled out a shoebox and set it on Melissa's lap. Melissa took off the lid and inside was a mess full of money. Crumpled and chaotic, dollar bills had been carelessly shoved into the box.

My eyes widened. I had never seen that much cash before. Trudy grabbed the box and emptied its contents on the bed between Melissa and I.

"Go ahead, count it," Trudy said.

Melissa and I looked at each other and without any more hesitation we began to sort and stack the bills.

"We'll give you both a little extra for helping us out." Trudy lit a cigarette and stood at the open door that faced the parking lot.

Melissa and I worked quickly. I wanted the extra money. I also wanted to get out of there.

"Four-hundred twenty dollars," Melissa said.

Trudy's boyfriend turned and pushed her shoulder. He began screaming in a different language. It was a strange language, not Spanish, I knew what that sounded like. German or Polish maybe. Trudy began sobbing. Melissa and I could only assume that the amount of money was far below what he expected. Trudy opened the door and motioned for Melissa and I to get in the van. Trudy drove us both home.

This routine of going to the motel, counting the money, Trudy's boyfriend screaming, her crying, and then Melissa and I getting dropped off, went on for a couple of weeks. I continued to go, and Trudy continued to pay me extra. Most weeks I made over $200. That was a fortune for a middle-schooler in the 1980s. It meant I could order pizza, get new clothes, and buy cigarettes. It meant that *He* couldn't steal my paychecks. I had cash.

Early August arrived and with it, a heat wave. Trudy decided to switch vehicles. "Just for you girls," she said the day she arrived in the pick-up truck. Melissa had already claimed the front seat with Trudy but on our way to work, I had squeezed myself in-between them. On the way home I sat in the uncovered bed of the pick-up truck. It was a relief from the stagnant air in the front of the truck. Trudy drove up to the curb in front of my house and before the truck came to a complete stop, I jumped onto my front lawn.

A quick snap jerked me back. I moved forward to steady myself, walked a few steps, and then fell. Trudy was already gone. I passed out on the front lawn. The next moment I remember was waking up in my bed. The night sky through my window told me it was very late at night or early in the morning. I was not sure what day it was. I tried to get up. Pain overwhelmed me, it radiated through my back and hip. My head began to throb.

I laid perfectly still until the sun began to shine through my window. I heard *His* footsteps approach my bed. I dared not move. The pain had made every muscle tense.

He sat down at the edge of my bed with a cup of medicine in *his* hand. "Take this," *He* said.

I struggled to lift my head but the thought of relief from the pain moved me without question. I swallowed the sticky liquid from the small cup. *He* stood up and moved to the end of the bed. *He* flung the covers off of my legs and grabbed my right ankle and knee. *He* curled *his* lips and smirked. *He* said nothing and then with a force I had never experienced, *he* twisted and wrenched my leg and hip. I felt a pop and then nothing.

I had dislocated my hip and for the next two weeks I existed in a state of foggy wake and sleep. Before and after *His* workday, *he* would visit with more medicine. Hazy visions of *him* in my doorway, on my bed, in my bed, all came and went until I slowly began to move and walk. I began practicing walking up and down the basement stairs. A week later, I started my first year in high school.

Chapter 37

Journal Entry from Me – July 11, 2018

So many mornings, too many mornings, I wake up feeling tired, stressed, and panicked. My nights are restless and terrifying, only to realize that it was a nightmare. I awake to the shadows next to my bed. Monsters there to rip me apart. I can smell the cigarettes on His clothes and on his breath. I can feel his course hands on my body. Not me. Not with him. The terror in the night belongs to them, how nice they are to share with me. Their experiences make me shrink like a neglected infant.

High School

High school was a whole new adventure. One I was not thrilled to take. I was popular and feared in middle school. I was nothing in high school. I started at the bottom with the rest of the incoming freshmen. I was one in a thousand. High school was hell.

The only friend that stuck with me in high school was Sarah. Her mother, a full-time, barely functioning alcoholic and truly heinous person, often traded Sarah to men for alcohol and rent money. In spite of my efforts to distance myself from Sarah, she was charming and forth-right, a refreshing change from the gossiping chattel in high school.

In middle school, *He* often begged me to bring friends home on weekends. *He* had a routine; get us drunk and then molest my friend. *He* would often bribe me with going out to eat, cash, or most of the time, it just made *him* happy and that was enough for me. I had some indication of what *he* was doing but none of my friends ever said anything. I often woke to find my friends in odd positions on my floor or crying. Some got quiet and called their parents to pick them up. I wasn't able to keep many friends, but Sarah was loyal, even if she was a little crazy.

The first month of school I quickly realized that *He* had been telling the truth all along; I was stupid. I was failing every class, even choir. I began skipping classes. Using any excuse to leave the classroom. I often hid in the bathroom for hours at a time. My classes were full of kids who were smart. I felt like they were watching me, judging me, they knew I was stupid. The teachers didn't waste any time calling on me for wrong answers. I often escaped by staring out the window.

Things changed when I met a new friend, Kate. She was friends with Sarah and had just moved back into the school district. They had been friends in Sarah's old neighborhood and the three of us began to hang out at Kate's house after school. Kate lived with her grandmother and three younger sisters. Their house was a tiny trailer in a run-down part of town. Kate was very short. She looked like she was only ten years old, but she was my age, thirteen. Kate had wiry brown hair and a small face. Her voice matched perfectly well with her physical features.

Sarah was never a fan of *Him*, and *he* knew it. *He* often told me *he* didn't want Sarah to come over, but I would sneak her home anyway. We drank vodka and talked about Sarah's mom's newest boyfriend and how he wouldn't leave her alone. Sarah seemed to have the same problem I did but her nightly visits were by different men. By the time high school came around, I got in trouble for everything and nothing at all. I figured I might as well do whatever I wanted; I was tired of the game.

One night *He* came home early from work and found Sarah sprawled out on the couch. I braced for the worst, but *he* didn't say anything. *He* grabbed a drink, sat in the recliner, lit a cigarette and watched the news on tv. I hurried to get Sarah off the couch and out the door.

"What the hell is she doing here?" *He* put *his* cigarette in the ash tray and looked over at me.

"Oh, she couldn't go home. She was supposed to go to Kate's but then her grandma said 'no,' and Sarah didn't have a place to go." My head dropped. "Sorry."

"Who's Kate?" *He* asked.

"A friend, I guess."

"Why not bring her over." *His* tone was light and kind. *His* lips curled into a smile.

"Um, I don't know if she can."

"Well, try," *He* stated.

He wanted Kate now. She was new and I was a worm on a hook.

Over the next few weeks, I made up excuses about why Kate couldn't come over, only to be followed by *His* comments about my disloyalty and weakness. Thanksgiving came and went. There were no family parties that year, at least none that included me. *He* kept a tight rein on the communication between me and my grandmother. I had always spent weekends and holidays with Grandma, but the past three years I had been secluded from outside family members. I had Sarah and Kate but family and teachers, according to *Him*, were the enemy. They asked too many questions.

Christmas break was approaching. The house grew cold and dark. Streaks of ice formed over the bathroom window. It was my last day of school before the new year. I stood at the mirror and brushed my thick wavy brown hair. I had stopped wearing make-up shortly after I began high school. The girls there found reasons to be cruel, but to be fair, I made it easy for them. I had taught myself to apply blue eyeshadow and dark red blush. Music videos were the new thing and the girls dancing on cars to rock music had been my tutors.

I was ready to go. I flung my backpack over one shoulder. My coat was a hand-me-down from *Him* and the zipper never worked. I grabbed both sides of the old grey coat and clenched them together. I opened the door to leave. My eyes stung as they met the winter air. It was still black outside. The moon had slipped away but the stars remained.

"Don't forget what I said," *His* voice echoed into the street. Startled, I half turned and nodded.

I walked quickly to the bus stop.

When I arrived at school, the halls were loud. Voices smashed together in a disorganized torturous symphony. It was a daily reminder of why I hated people. I had my two friends and everyone else had quietly stepped away. I was a freak. My middle school days were filled with fun girly things. High school had turned me into a burn-out. I wore an old man's coat, flannel shirts that were three sizes too big, and pants that had crept up my legs by three inches. I had no money left from my summer job. I couldn't buy new clothes or make-up, *He* had taken and spent the last of my cash as I healed from the injury a few months before. The only relief I had was the endless supply of vodka waiting for me every afternoon.

The first bell range. Kids hurried to their first class. I hadn't made it to my locker yet. I couldn't remember where it was. Lost again, I would miss my first hour by hiding out in the bathroom. Most classes I locked myself in a stall and read the social studies book, or at least pretended. *I was stupid*. I didn't understand any of it. I managed to make it to the next two class periods. At lunch, I found Sarah and Kate.

"Hey guys!"

Still wearing my winter coat and backpack, I sat down at the long table next to Kate.

"Hey, so like, my dad said if you want to come over during Christmas break you totally can. *He* said we could go to the bowling alley or something."

Knowing how Sarah felt about *Him*, I directed my conversation only to Kate.

"That sounds cool. I gotta talk to my nana about it though."

"Cool."

"Could *he* give me a ride?" Kate pulled out an apple and gave it to me.

"Yeah, probably."

Unsure if it was jealousy over not being asked or anger for Kate's ignorance about *Him*, Sarah darted her eyes at Kate. Sarah grunted, "whatever," picked up her lunch tray and tossed it in the trash. I wouldn't see Sarah again until the next summer.

A few days later, Kate called and said she could come over New Year's Eve weekend. When I told *Him* Kate could come, *he* said we could go get her the next day. We picked Kate up on a Saturday and she planned to stay until Monday, New Year's Day.

We arrived at Kate's trailer. *He* got out of the car and knocked on the door. Her grandma answered the door in her bath robe and seemed surprised that *He* would want talk to her. I'm not sure what *he* said, but Kate's grandma smiled and waved as we pulled away.

"We need to make a quick stop," *He* said. *He* pulled the minivan into the parking lot of the corner drugstore. "Come on."

Kate and I followed *him* into the store. *He* said, "get anything you want."

He pushed the small cart to us, "snacks, games, whatever." *He* smiled and made *his* way to the beverage section. "You girls want anything to drink? I know this one likes her vodka." *He* gave me a wink and then turned and picked up various bottles of liquor.

Kate giggled, "how about a Screwdriver?" With her childlike voice and stature, it was difficult to take her seriously.

"Well, that makes it easy, we already vodka at home. I'll get a little more just in case." *He* looked at me, knowing I had emptied one gallon already and the other was almost gone. "You, grab some orange juice, not the shitty stuff, the real orange juice."

The checkout clerk didn't ask any questions. Kate and I laughed and talked about how much fun it would be to play Candy Land while drunk. Once home, we unpacked our sugary snacks, vodka, tequila, orange juice, and Candy Land.

He went into the living room, turned on the television and told us we were going to watch a movie first. "You need some help there?" *He* called out as Kate twisted off the cap to the vodka and orange juice.

"Nope. Got it," Kate called back. She proceeded to pour three glasses of mostly vodka with a fraction of orange juice. I was used to straight vodka. The orange juice was minimal but tasted good.

Kate and I walked into the living room, and I handed *Him* a glass. *He* put it on the end table and said, "Sit. Watch." I took my spot on the floor. Kate seemed confused but followed my lead and sat next to me. A black and white version of Dracula played. The vodka helped dampen the blaring sound effects from the movie.

I fumbled to find my glass on the floor. I realized it was empty and noticed that Kate had disappeared too. Her empty glass was next to mine, but she had found her way to the couch where *He* was sitting. She was slumped over *his* lap. My stomach sank. Had I fallen asleep? When did she get there? *Shit!*

I got to my feet and walked to the couch, "time for bed, come on." I pulled Kate's arm. I pulled hard and half of her body fell to the floor. "Come on, it's time for bed!" *He* grabbed her torso and pulled her back to *his* lap. We were stuck in a tug of war. I didn't let go. I pulled again. She fell to the floor.

"Get the fuck out of here!" *He* shouted!

I tried one more time. *He* lunged forward, put her on the couch and began to take off *his* belt.

"I'm going, okay, I'm going."

I let go of Kate's arm and went to my room. I was empty. She was on her own. I left the door cracked. I thought maybe she would wake up and come to bed. A while later I heard footsteps thudding down the hall. It was *Him*. Through the crack in my door, I saw H*im* carry Kate's limp body toward *his* bedroom. She looked so small. Her stringy hair swung as *he* struggled to get *his* door open. Once inside *his* room, I heard the familiar sounds of *his* comforter, soft moans, the cries of a little girl, grunting, and then nothing.

The next morning, I woke to find Kate on my bedroom floor. She was dressed in one of my nightgowns and staring at the ceiling. She was awake but didn't speak for hours.

Without saying a word, Kate, and I both got dressed.

"Let's go," *He* called out.

"What? Where?" I asked.

"I told you I would take you to the bowling alley. Let's go," *he* said.

I was relieved at the chance to get out of the

house but also confused. *He* never kept *his* promises.

    Kate stayed silent until we arrived at the bowling alley. The building was locked, it was Sunday, and we were four hours too early. Kate and I spent the next two hours walking around the parking lot and the woods behind the building. We sat on large rocks that graced the entrance. It was there that Kate told me what happened. She didn't tell me everything. I didn't let on that I already knew what *He* had done; what I had done. *He* persuaded me to bring her home, sometimes with a belt and other times with warm accolades. I was weak and useless. *He* used me to get to her. I was getting too old. I looked too much like a woman. Kate looked like a little girl.

    A few days passed. Kate had returned home, and I was left with *Him*, though not entirely. *He* went back to work while Christmas break was happening for me. *I wondered if she had told her nana.* My mind raced. Sarah wasn't answering the phone and I was too ashamed to call Kate. My days and afternoons were spent alone. *His* schedule was predictable and so was mine. Get up in the morning while *he* was still sleeping, clean the house, watch tv, listen to the radio, and stay in my room until *he* went to work. *He* was only awake for an hour or two before leaving and then returned after midnight. *He* stayed awake most of the night, sometimes, I did too.

I returned to school the following Monday and made no attempt to find my locker or first class. I went straight to the office. I was compelled by unfamiliar voices screaming to tell someone, anyone. I burst into the counselor's office and sat down in front of him.

"Hi!" Mr. Collins said. He was the school counselor. He was short and robust in the middle. He raised one eyebrow and asked, "how can I help you?"

Mr. Collins was known to be kind, but I hadn't yet known it for myself. He took off his reading glasses and put down the papers he was holding. I couldn't breathe. I panicked.

"I have to go." I scooped up my backpack and coat.

"Wait a minute," he said. "Come on back. Tell me what's happening."

I sat down and blurted out with sarcasm,

"hypothetically speaking what would happen if your dad had sex with your friend?" He stared at me. "You know, hypothetically." I quipped.

The next several minutes I told in detail what I knew about Christmas break, alcohol, *Him*, and Kate. I said everything that happened that weekend and nothing more. Kate's story had nothing to do with me. I wasn't telling about me and *Him*, it was Kate and *Him*. I dreamt up the justifications in my mind as I spoke. *He* wouldn't know it was me who told. What if Kate said something too? I would blame her. She told. It wasn't me. The thoughts swirled in my head.

The next two weeks I was empty. I had let go of a secret. I didn't know how to put it back in. I remained silent at home and school. I missed every class and even the bus several times, requiring *Him* to pick me up. *He* became perplexed by the change in demeaner, lack of bathing, and wearing four-day old clothes.

One ride home from school resulted in an awkward discussion about *his* suspicions over my sexual preferences. "Are you a lesbian?" *He* asked so casually.

"No."

Absolute in my response, *he* said, "okay, just wondering because … you know," *he* made gesture toward my outfit and lifted my hair and quickly dropped it. *His* acknowledgement of my dirty appearance stirred up anger. *What the hell does he care? Sick.*

Two days later at 4:26 PM, the phone range. Thinking it was Sarah, I quickly answered.

"Hello?"

"Is this Amy?" Not Sarah, it was a man's voice on the phone.

"Yeah, this is Amy."

"Do you know your father's been arrested today?"

Time stopped.

"Hello?" The man's voice cut the air. "Are

you there?"

"Hon, pack a bag and give me a name and number of someone who can pick you up."

"Okay." I robotically responded and began do what he said. I desperately wanted my grandmother. My stomach sank. Full of shame, I thought, *she can't know*. In the end, *everyone* knew.

I went to the kitchen, grabbed the emergency contact card, and returned to the phone in my bedroom. It was the name and number of friends of the family, though I hadn't seen them in years. I hung up the phone, grabbed a duffle bag from the closet and began filling it with clothes and stuffed animals. I thought, *I'll run away. I'm dead anyway. Just run.*

I couldn't think of a plan fast enough. There was nowhere to go, no one else to call, and then a knock on the door. *Shit, I need a shower.* I went to the door and let in Mary. She had been a friend of the family for several years but I called her my aunt. She hugged me and said we had to hurry.

"Can I take a shower?" I felt defeated and disgusted with the way I smelled. "Please?"

"No, we have to go. You can a shower when we get home."

Home? I looked around, not knowing it would be last time I would be in that house. That day was the last day I would attend my high school, the last day I would hide out in a bathroom stall, the last day I took a swig of vodka, and the last day I saw *his* bed.

I didn't take a shower when I arrived at my aunt's, I went to bed in the spare room and slept, hard. The next morning, I heard voices from the living room. They resonated through the floor of the spare room. Sharp pains stabbed my chest. It was *His* voice I heard.

"Amy!" my aunt called for me.

The only bathroom was downstairs, and I had to go pee, bad. I wouldn't be able to get there without seeing *Him*. I didn't understand why *he* was there. *He* was in jail yesterday. I slowly made my way downstairs and headed straight to the bathroom. Without moving my head, I could see *his* legs. *He* was sitting on the couch. I took as much as time as I could in the bathroom, trying to wipe off a week's worth of stink and dirt. I took a deep breath, came out and stood in the kitchen.

"Come here," *He* patted the spot on the couch next to *him*. Noticing only the floor and trying not to kick the dog that kept walking in front of me, I sat down next to *him*.

"Happy to see me?" *He* asked.

"Yeah," I managed to say.

Inaudible conversation between *Him* and my aunt was interrupted by *his* hand on my thigh. There were no windows in my aunt's house. There were paintings, shelves, and knickknacks. No windows.

"Did you hear me?" *He* asked.

I turned my head toward *him*. My eyes were focused on *his* mouth. "You ruined my fucking life."

I turned my head back to the painting on the wall. No windows.

He was charged with first degree sexual

assault but there was no trial. *He* pled guilty to a lesser charge and only served one year in the county jail. The next two years I lived with my aunt and her family. Every day over the next few years brought new challenges. I was stuck in a tornado of events over which I had no control. I had a new family, a new school, new friends, and new addictions. That story is for another time.

Chapter 38

National Conference 2019

Walking through the corridors of a major university, today is the first day of the annual anti-trafficking conference. This conference I had been to several times. This was the third time I had been asked to speak. It is three days of breakout sessions, new faces, unique jewelry and bags to buy at the vendor tables; all made in foreign countries by survivors of human trafficking of course. The air reminded me of my days in college. I miss the smell of old books and musty carpet. I don't miss the maze of halls and long walks from one lecture hall to the next. I am hopelessly directionally challenged, even indoors.

Sitting down in the cafeteria, where the last session was held, I had some time to reflect on the day's *activities. I wrote V a little summary.*

"I spoke yesterday and told my story,

again. It went well but I'm glad today was all about soaking in new information from others. My first session was all about assessment in healthcare, which is so relevant to work we're already doing. We may have an opportunity to help the medical community here develop training and protocol. My second session was so super cool because it focused on therapeutic interventions with people who have experienced trafficking. The biggest focus was on relationship-building and holding space for the client to heal, to BE! So YOU! They also emphasized helping clients re-write their narrative, it's helpful to know what the narrative is first, but still. The next session was a complete waste of time. I thought it was going to be more about how to develop assessment and protocol for immigrants, but it was so basic. Everyone in the room was so bored. I kind of felt bad for the speaker. Everything she was saying, we pretty much already knew.

The best session was the one on prevention. It was a research study and it confirmed everything we have been doing is exactly what we should be doing. I know we can do more, and I plan on implementing what I can, but I am also more committed than

*ever to get this program into the school
system, for the teachers first, then we can
address self-worth and esteem strategies with
youth, but the teachers have to buy-in first."*

I looked up from pen and notebook in time to
see that two people had joined me at the table. In the
far back of the room and closest to the door, I had
expected to keep this table to myself. I gently laid my
head down on my notebook and closed my eyes for a
moment. A voice rang out from the speakers, "check,
check, check." The next, and final speaker was
getting ready to take the stage. I straightened myself
out as best I could and politely smiled. A tall lanky
woman, quite plain looking, no makeup, wearing
jeans and a flannel shirt took the microphone from the
technician and cleared her throat. She had a small,
quiet voice. She grimaced at the bright lights, and I
leaned in.

The woman tugged at the bottom of her shirt,
looked straight ahead and began talking. She told us
of her time growing up in a small rural town in the
mid-west. Her father was the leader of the local
Masons and their religious community. The men in
the group were encouraged to bring their children to

her home where the meetings were held. Strong
threats of Hell and damnation compelled entire
families to keep in close contact with her father; the
only one who could save their souls and keep them
accountable. Once indoctrinated, men would prove
their loyalty by forcing this woman, who at the time
was only three years old, to do horrendous sexual acts
on them and they on her. Burning candles, incense,
and chanting were all part of the weekly rituals and
more and more men came and brought their own
children.

The scenes were familiar, I was in it with her
and yet in my own body, I felt ashamed and scared.
Wasn't she afraid? He is going to find her. My mind
raced with thoughts of *Him* walking through the door.
Just listening to this was a violation. *He* will know
and find me, trouble. My body burned and ached.
Something was crawling out from the inside and I
couldn't release it. I can't leave now; everyone will
see me. *Stay until the end*, I told myself.

The woman said the abuse stopped when she
was thirteen years old, when her father was caught
and went to prison. *How ironic*, I thought. The same
age as me when my father went to jail. I was relieved
to know her father would never get her again, he was
in prison for a very long time, not the case with mine,

he can still find me. *He will find me*.

     Nobody moved from the tables, even after she finished her story. Two hundred sitting statues, immovable and in shock, I wanted desperately to retreat but did not want to be the first one out of my seat. There was one more event after this, I was planning to go but decided to head back to the hotel. People began to stir, and I took my chance. I packed my notebook and pen in my bag and left.

     The hotel was in a very bad part of town, but the price was right. The best thing was that it had an indoor pool. A quick snack and I was ready for a swim. My toes hit the water and I felt calm. I slowly walked down the steps and fully submersed myself into the warm water. I swam to the end and then quickly to the other. I did this over and over as if I was in a race. I'm not a great swimmer but no one was watching. With every move, little pieces of whatever had been trying to crawl out of me began to shed itself into the water. Time had no meaning and I watched as the sun set through the massive windows. Empty, I floated.

     The next day, while still at the hotel, I opened my laptop and saw emails from the night before. Mimi and Anna sometimes take matters into their own hands. They yearn for connection and love, and they have it with V. It read "mommmymommmymommy," over and over again, followed by hearts and happy face emojis. Several lines of Mimi's crying out for "mommy," and Anna writes, "it's Anna, but the mommy stuff is all from Mimi, it's funny because it says 'mommy' and 'my mom' too."

My heart dropped. The thought of such boldness felt reckless, but my angst quickly disappeared when I opened my email and read V's response. Tears fell. V wrote, "Hi Anna and Mimi, you both touch my heart so much and it is lovely to think of you as daughters. I am holding you both when we are together and when we are apart."

Chapter 39

Last Chapter - Maybe

My story didn't end when He went to jail. A new story began. This has been the pattern of my life for as long as I can remember. Having the courage to tell did not turn out the way I had hoped. Though I don't know that I hoped for anything, I just needed to tell.

Life may have turned out differently if the several people who knew what was happening at the time, used their courage to tell. They didn't and it wasn't until I was thirteen years old that I realized no one was coming to save me. I learned that lesson early and it has stuck. When I get the chance to tell the truth, I do. When I get the chance to change someone's life for the better, I do. I'm not always popular because of it but I am better for it, I don't know any other way.

After *He* went to jail, the people who were

charged with caring for me, kept me in *his* life. Whether out of naivety or greed, *He* remained in my life for eight more years. Much of this book is changed because *he* is still alive. I don't want *him* to know what we've written this book. I don't want *him* to know how much I remember, despite *his* best efforts to call it a dream, and me a liar. Part of me, or perhaps even *parts* of me, still feel the shame for outing *him*, shame for being jealous over *his* young victims, and shame that this body carries the memories of events long past, yet present.

Many parts participated in the creation of this book. There are little ones who remain in the background, watching. They are no less a part of this process than the Professional who is determined to learn and educate on childhood trauma. She is determined to excel in the field of psychology and social services in a way that sheds a light on familial sexual abuse and trafficking. Her relentless pursuit of education has provided all of us with multiple degrees, published books, and speaking opportunities.

He tried to break us and, I suppose in a very real sense, *he* did. We are in pieces but not broken. Every trauma that resulted in a new part, showed up to save the whole of us and we thrive because of it. *He* tried to break us, that's true. What *he* did was create a fortress, each wall built because of trauma, and made of the strongest energy the universe has to offer. No, we did not break. We grew. We adapted. We lived to tell the story.

Today

I hear the birds singing outside the window. They have decided my lawn is their favorite place today. They have come to visit in large flocks, tiny black dots pecking at the ground. The sun warms my feet, I have propped them up on a box under my desk. Ah, my desk, my new, beautiful writing desk. A friend gifted it to me. It is my new tool and offers an element of elegance to my simple home.

My life is beautiful now. Not perfect or without struggle but it offers me a place to rest, some peace against the difficulties of my memories. I know where I have come from and it's ugly and dark, at least a large portion of it. But it's also full of rich characters and stories. It's full of love and connection. My life wouldn't be what it is if other parts had not saved me from the events of what was. The capacity to relinquish oneself, to become someone else is a remarkable gift only given to those of us who truly need it. Being a multiple is other worldly. It defies the imagination and can hardly be explained by one who carries the other parts within them. They are me and I am them. We are linked, not mashed together as one, and that will never be the goal. To know each other's memories, the hurts, the joys, the relationships, is to know me but I will always remain a "we."

What I've come to know by writing this chapter in our lives is that God was there. He was with me and all of the little ones. God wept with us in the night. God was in the closet with Mimi and in the shadows with Six. He was with Eight in the basement. He was with Iggy in the truck. God was with us the whole time. I've come to accept that in the midst of it all God saw me, knew me, and through all my shame continued to love me.

My thoughts turn to V. She has been a constant in my life for several years now. She knows all of us better than I do, and she continues to show her compassion and love for even the unlovable parts. We are grateful for her love, her unconditional regard, and continued support for our healing. Thank you, V!

About the Author

Amy Joy is a graduate from the University of Michigan. She has earned a bachelor's degree in social work and a master's degree in public administration. Her current ventures include earning a PhD in psychology. She continues to work with at-risk populations and educates professionals on how to appropriately identify and respond to trauma-related challenges in individuals and communities. Amy's published works include *Human Trafficking 101: Stories, Stats, and Solutions* and *Write Your Story: A Guided Journal for Healing Trauma*. She currently resides in Michigan with her two cats, George and Kiki, and of course, her scrappy dog, Sully.

Amy is often invited to speak at national and local conferences. If you or your agency would like Amy to speak at your next event, please visit **www.amyjoypresents.com**.

Amy Joy anticipates the next book to be released in the Spring of 2023.

For current and future publications, please visit **www.amyjoypresents.com**.